"So you're basically an adrenaline junkie?"

"You bet. Nothing like a shot of endorphins to get the blood pumping." He crooked a finger and she leaned closer. "Throw in a kick of dopamine and serotonin and you're on a high almost as good as…" His pupils widened as he trailed off, giving her fair indication what he'd been about to say.

The safe thing to do would be to change the subject. But she'd done safe her entire life and hadn't it only been a day ago when she'd arrived in Melbourne that she'd vowed to loosen up? To start living a little?

Yeah, she'd had a gutful of safe.

"As good as…?"

She held her breath as a flicker of lust lit a spark to his eyes, a flash of caramel in all that gorgeous brown.

"Sex."

NICOLA MARSH has always had a passion for writing and reading. As a youngster she devoured books when she should have been sleeping, and later kept a diary whose content could be an epic in itself! These days, when she's not enjoying life with her husband and son in her home city of Melbourne, she's at her computer, creating the romances she loves in her dream job. Visit Nicola's website, www.nicolamarsh.com, for the latest news of her books.

Other titles by Nicola Marsh available in ebook:

Harlequin Presents® Extra

INTERVIEW WITH THE DAREDEVIL

NICOLA MARSH

~ Unbuttoned by a Rebel ~

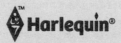

Harlequin®

TORONTO NEW YORK LONDON
AMSTERDAM PARIS SYDNEY HAMBURG
STOCKHOLM ATHENS TOKYO MILAN MADRID
PRAGUE WARSAW BUDAPEST AUCKLAND

Recycling programs
for this product may
not exist in your area.

ISBN-13: 978-0-373-52855-4

INTERVIEW WITH THE DAREDEVIL

First North American Publication 2012

Copyright © 2011 by Nicola Marsh

www.Harlequin.com

Printed in U.S.A.

Dear Reader,

There are some magical places on earth that inspire books. The Taj Mahal, the Eiffel Tower, the Statue of Liberty…books set in Agra and Paris and New York are memorable.

For me, personally researching the stories I write can help the words flow. Visiting the luxurious Palazzo Versace on the Gold Coast certainly did that.

The opulent surroundings sparked my imagination to the extent I wrote the bulk of this book in a week when I returned home, my head filled with images of marble and mosaic and a spa that absolutely had to have its own scene in the book.

For my heroine Ava, spending time at an amazing hotel is balm for her battered soul— though that could have more to do with extreme sports adventurer Roman, whose easy smiles and irrepressible roguishness have her falling in love for the first time.

I love a hero who brings out the best in a heroine.

I hope you do, too.

Happy reading,

Nicola

With thanks to the brilliant staff at Palazzo Versace, who were smiling & enthusiastic & helpful while I researched this book. I'll be back!

CHAPTER ONE

Ava Beckett sighed with pleasure as she slid into the warm water, lazily breast-stroking to the edge of the infinity pool where she propped on her forearms, staring out at the lights of Melbourne glittering twenty-seven floors below.

She'd stayed at luxurious hotels around the world but there was something decadently edgy and funky about Melbourne's newest, the Crown Metropol.

Sighing at the self-indulgence of having the pool all to herself, she let go of the side and floated on her back, eyes closed.

How often had she done this? Done absolutely nothing? Try never. Being the prime minister's daughter had been bad enough, being a diplomat's wife harder. Every minute of every day scheduled to a second: what she wore, what she did, what she ate and when. Stifling. Suffocating. Strangling.

Opening her eyes, she focused on the water's reflection shimmering across the roof, happy to do nothing but float. That or pinch herself to see if all this was real, for she still had a hard time believing she was free.

Finally.

Her relationship with Leon had lasted ten years, their lacklustre marriage two, yet the public fallout from their divorce over the last month had been what shattered her most. Every scandalous, invented word plastered across newspapers and magazines making her life hell.

So she'd escaped. Ditched Canberra for Melbourne, abbreviated her surname to Beck and checked into a new hotel in blessed anonymity.

She needed this break to recover from having her name vilified by muck-raking journalists hell-bent on selling copy rather than the truth, needed some private time to savour her freedom without looking over her shoulder for fear of a long-range lens intruding on a moment that could be misconstrued.

She'd been photographed swimming, grocery shopping and heading into a zumba class, three perfectly innocuous, everyday pastimes not allowed by recently divorced women apparently. They'd cast her as frivolous, callous, cold-blooded; and that had been the nice reporters.

She knew why they'd latched onto her after the divorce while leaving Leon unscathed, but it didn't make it any easier. Shying away from answering questions, preferring to maintain a poised front and take a back seat to her famous father and extroverted husband over the years had been misconstrued as aloofness and arrogance whereas Leon's easy smiles and garrulousness made him the media's darling.

She'd been hounded and chased and bruised by the smear campaign over her divorce and she was done.

Time to take control of her life and moving to Melbourne ensured that; if she stayed under the radar.

A soft splash nearby created a gentle wave but the slight disturbance tossing her off kilter didn't bother her. In fact, a tidal wave probably wouldn't shake this surreal feeling of liberating independence.

Bumping against the side of the pool, she rolled over to swim a few laps and promptly crashed into someone, their heads colliding in a sickening clash.

Seeing stars, she submerged, grateful for a strong pair of hands around her waist hauling her upwards.

'You okay?'

Mortified as she coughed and spluttered before finding her voice, she nodded, swiping hair out of her eyes.

'Yeah, fine,' she croaked at the same instant she caught sight of her rescuer—and promptly choked again.

Maybe she'd bumped her head too hard for she could've sworn her rescuer, the guy still holding her, was George Clooney.

'Must have a hard head,' he said, his lips curving into a devastating smile that had her chest constricting, making her breathless as she wondered whether she'd swallowed water.

That had to be the reason behind her breathlessness.

Flustered, she pointed to his head. 'Could say the same about yours.'

'Touché.'

His smile faded as concern darkened his brown eyes to ebony.

'Are you really okay? I could ring for an ice pack? Or walk you back to your room?'

Incredulous, Ava shook her head, instantly regretting it as a sharp pain jabbed her skull where she'd connected with his.

'Tell me this wasn't some lame pickup.'

Confusion creased his brow and she breathed a sigh of relief before he laughed, a deep, full chuckle that rippled over her skin like warm treacle.

'Let me assure you, I can think of smoother ways to ask a beautiful woman out than taking her to Casualty.'

'The bump wasn't that bad,' she said, probing her skull and wincing when her fingertips brushed the lump, and he immediately reached up.

'Let me.'

Amazingly, she did, stilling as he slid his fingers into her hair, savouring the electric thrill that shot through her at his gentleness.

She held her breath as his fingertips slid over the bump, considerate, exploring and as she lifted her gaze to meet his something inexplicable happened.

Her body buzzed to life.

In a *big* way.

Must've been some bump, she thought as she belatedly realised their intimate position: his hand spanning her waist, holding her close, his other sliding around the back of her head, cupping it, their bodies wet and slick and almost touching.

She hadn't been this close to a guy in a long time and she almost squirmed like a puppy having its tummy rubbed.

'Feels nasty. Maybe you should rest on one of the lounges for a while?'

She managed a mute nod, trying not to whimper with pleasure as his fingers slid out of her hair, brushing it back out of her face.

There was something sweetly sensual in the slow sweep of his hand as it smoothed her hair behind her ears, giving her an unimpeded view of a hard, tanned chest that must've seen dumb-bells on a daily basis.

By the smattering of dark hair he wasn't one of those waxed gym junkies, and she immediately wondered why she'd noticed or cared.

'Let me give you a hand.'

Annoyed she'd been blatantly staring, she raised her gaze to his and if he weren't steadying her with one hand around her waist she would've gone under, for what she saw in those dark chocolate eyes wasn't the concern of a stranger.

Uh-uh, what she saw in those mesmerising depths mirrored the same, irrational hunger making her want to do crazy things. Things like wrapping her legs around his waist, like sliding her hands all over that muscular chest, like encouraging him to hoist her onto the edge of the pool and kiss her senseless.

'Come on.' He cleared his throat but not before his huskiness told her he'd probably read every embarrassing thought she'd just had.

She'd been taught from a young age to shield her thoughts, to ensure her face gave away nothing. Her dad had drummed it home about the dangers of lurking paparazzi, of long-range scopes on high-tech cameras, so she'd spent her life hiding her feelings behind a carefully constructed mask of impassivity. A mask that had well and truly slipped in the joy of floating in this pool after her hellish month, and in the joy of fantasising after landing in this guy's arms.

'How's your head?'

'I'll live.' He winked as they reached the stairs and she could've sworn her heart tripped up the steps ahead of her. 'Besides, if I suddenly go into cardiac arrest you can give me mouth-to-mouth.'

Not used to flirting but dying to get back in the game, she pretended to study his heart, which basically gave her another excuse to ogle that impressive chest.

Tapping her bottom lip, she pretended to ponder. 'Isn't mouth-to-mouth only given if you stop breathing?'

'In that case, that happened about five minutes ago.'

She couldn't help it; she blushed.

Marrying a family friend straight out of university hadn't exactly endowed her with femme fatale skills. Her relationship with Leon had been comfortable and familiar, devoid of sparks or flirtation. She'd never learned how but she had a feeling if she hung around this pool much longer she'd be given a crash course by an expert.

'I think I can take it from here.'

She took a step and stumbled, making a mockery of her attempt at asserted independence and only serving to have him touch her again when his arm shot out and locked around her waist.

'Easy, you may have a slight concussion.'

There was nothing slight about it; it was the only explanation behind her letting him lead her to one of the double bed chaises and insisting she lie down—with him beside her.

Increasingly self-conscious of her wet high-cut navy one-piece and pebbling skin, she tried to sit up and reach for her robe but he was one step ahead of her.

'Here.'

He held it up and as she slid her arms into the hotel's thick, plush dove-grey robe she shivered, not from the cold but from the unexpected tenderness from a stranger as he belted it just right.

'Better?'

She nodded, easing back onto the pillows at the insistence of his gentle hands.

'You can go now.'

Her words sounded harsh, especially after how kind he'd been but she needed space, needed him to not lie next to her, needed him to be rude and obnoxious rather than easy-going and likeable.

For lying here next to a sexy, kind stranger beside a deserted infinity pool on the top floor of a chic hotel reeked of adventure and daring and romance, three things that couldn't be more alien.

'Wish I could, but I can't.'

He rolled onto his side and propped on his elbow, looking like a poster boy for jump-starting women's libidos: long, lean, tanned, muscular and dripping wet, with a pair of mid-thigh board shorts moulding to...

She gulped and dragged her gaze upwards, meeting the twinkling in his eyes only marginally better.

'It's my duty to see you're okay. Concussions are serious business.' He tapped his head. 'Trust me, I know, I've had enough of them.'

Intrigued, she wriggled into the pillows, sat up a little higher.

'Occupational hazard?'

His mouth kicked into a wicked smile that made her belly flip.

'You could say that.'

Well aware chatting would only encourage him to stay rather than leave she had a momentary battle with her inner well-trained marionette, the one that had told her to sit up straighter and keep her opinions to herself.

In the face of his devastating smile and those liquid chocolate eyes, the battle was over before it began.

'What do you do?'

'I'm in extreme sports.'

'In?'

He laughed at her obvious confusion. 'I'm CEO of the governing body for extreme sports worldwide. Heard of action sport? Adventure sport?'

Action? Adventure? Two things that couldn't be further from the sedate, sheltered, proper life she'd led.

'You mean stuff like bungee jumping?'

'And the rest.'

His face lit up and she admired his enthusiasm for his work. She'd never had it, the boring number crunching at the merchant bank less than inspiring. Quitting her job not long after quitting her marriage had been another faux pas according to the vigilante press.

'Tell me about your job.'

'Sure you're interested?'

She nodded, increasingly intrigued. Action, adventure, *extreme*, encapsulated a lifestyle she could only dream about. What would it be like to live life on the edge? To take risks? To never have to worry about what other people thought of you?

She'd never known but for this brief, surreal interlude with a guy she'd never see again she could live vicariously for a while.

'Yeah, tell me about the dangerous speeds and hair-raising heights and stunts you do for a living.'

'So you do know about extreme sports.'

Her hand wavered. 'A little.'

When he raised an eyebrow, she shrugged. 'I may have caught a few events in a competition on television last summer.'

'Go on, admit it, you were dying to hang-glide and wake-board.'

His animation snatched her breath and she unconsciously leaned forward.

'Considering I like both feet firmly on the ground, that would be a resounding *no*, but it was cool watching competitors battle environmental challenges while competing against each other.'

'Wind, snow, water, mountains, you name it, we do it.'

'So you're basically an adrenalin junkie?'

She made it sound as though he killed cockroaches for a living but he didn't mind, the crinkles at the corners of his eyes deepening; by the creases her rescuer spent a lot of time laughing.

'You bet. Nothing like a shot of endorphins to get the blood pumping.'

He crooked a finger and she leaned closer. 'Throw in a kick of dopamine and serotonin and you're on a high almost as good as...'

His pupils widened as he trailed off, giving her fair indication what he'd been about to say.

The safe thing to do would be to change the subject. But she'd done safe her entire life and hadn't it only been a day ago when she'd arrived in Melbourne that she'd vowed to loosen up? To start living a little?

Yeah, she'd had a gutful of safe.

'As good as?'

She held her breath as a flicker of lust lit a spark to his eyes, a flash of caramel in all that gorgeous brown.

'Sex.'

He didn't blink, didn't look away and she could've sworn the invisible thread binding them tugged.

The flirt's response would be 'that good, huh?' but she'd used up her limited chutzpah supply in the last few seconds.

Besides, the thought of sex being anything other than routine and lacklustre was as foreign to her as this guy and his extreme sports.

'What else do you do besides skydive and snowboard and cliff diving?'

He chuckled at her sidestep. 'You really want to hear

about nine air sports, eighteen land sports and fifteen water sports?'

'Maybe not.' Impressed by his mile-wide daredevil streak, she shook her head. 'You seriously do all that stuff?'

'Yeah, all that and more.'

He paused, his gaze momentarily flicking to her lips. 'Much more.'

And just like that the thread binding them tugged harder, like an intangible, irresistible force dragging her towards him.

'Are you impressed?'

'I think you're crazy,' she blurted, wondering if she could've picked anyone more different to while away a few minutes.

'So I've been told,' he said, not in the least offended by her outburst. 'What do you do for kicks?'

In that moment the drudgery of her life flashed before her eyes: being the daughter of the prime minister, the private school, the chauffeurs, the bodyguards, the etiquette and deportment lessons, the expected marriage, being a politician's wife, the civilised divorce no matter what lies the press printed.

All of it, every constrained, uptight second of it rose up to suffocate her, as it had her entire life.

But she wouldn't put up with it. Not any more. She needed to wipe those memories, needed to start creating new ones.

Starting now.

'What do I do for kicks?'

Buoyed by his talk of adrenalin and a soul-deep craving to let loose, she lay her hands on his shoulders and tugged him towards her, murmuring, 'This,' a second before her lips touched his.

CHAPTER TWO

THE moment Ava's lips touched the sexy stranger's she deliberately blotted out every sane reason why she shouldn't be doing this and simply allowed herself to *feel*.

His warmth was the first thing she noticed, the heat from his lips moulding hers, melting, mesmerising, as she moved her mouth experimentally against his.

In response his hand slid into her hair, cradling the back of her head but this time there was nothing remotely gentle or therapeutic in his touch.

Uh-uh, this time his fingers splayed and pulled her towards him while his skilled mouth coaxed hers into opening.

As his tongue touched hers starbursts exploded in her head as she belatedly wondered if she *had* sustained a concussion.

Surely that could be the only explanation for this dazed, stunned confusion clouding her usually immaculate rationale and making her want to kiss a guy she barely knew for ever.

Yeah, he was *that* good and when the pressure of his lips eased she wanted to scream 'no-o-o!'

For this was when her reliable logic would kick in, the logic that had helped her breeze through tense seat-ing arrangements at foreign embassies, the logic that had prompted her to give up her writing dream and undertake a sensible economics degree, the logic that had insisted marrying a family friend would be a solid basis for a sound marriage.

Screw logic.

'Can I blame that on concussion?'

The lips she'd just ravaged kicked up at the corners. 'That depends.'

'On?'

'How bad it is.'

With a fake wince, she pointed to her head and pretended to swoon. 'It's beyond bad.'

'In that case, I insist I walk you to your room.'

His gaze dropped to her mouth for a moment. 'Just in case you impulsively kiss every stranger you come into contact with.'

Just like that, her bubble of illusion popped. For that was what she'd done. Kissed a stranger, some random guy, she'd met in a hotel.

Sheesh. What had she been thinking? It was one thing to abandon boring logic, another to lose sight of the facts completely.

'Hey, I was kidding.'

He touched her arm and a spark of something zapped her, reminding her of the reason she'd ignored logic in the first place.

'Though introducing ourselves should take care of the stranger problem?'

He smiled and her chest constricted. Smooth, sweet-talking charmers shouldn't have a lethal smile too.

'Roman. Extreme sports fanatic.'

He held out his hand. 'And part-time poolside paramedic.'

She laughed, the carefree cadence foreign to her ears. When was the last time she'd laughed, really laughed, just for the heck of it?

Not while living in Canberra under Daddy's watchful eye while he'd stood at Australia's helm, not during her sedate two-year marriage and certainly not during her divorce last month, a divorce that had been publicly scrutinised while her name had been dragged through the mud for no other reason than she was Ava Beckett, reported society royalty, who'd supposedly got what was coming to her.

It felt good, great in fact, and by those attractive crinkles at the corners of his eyes Roman had spent a hell of a lot more time than she had laughing.

She placed her hand in his. 'Ava. Recent quitter of boring financier job. Clumsy oaf and danger to others poolside.'

His fingers closed over hers, his grip firm and solid, and another little shiver of awareness slithered through her.

'Well, then, with your clumsiness and my paramedic skills, we're a match made in heaven.'

He squeezed her hand and released it when she grimaced.

'Tell me those lines don't usually work for you.'

He leaned closer and she bit her lip at the sudden onslaught of masculinity temptingly within reach. 'You tell me?'

Sotto voce, combined with a wink, had her laughing again.

'So when you're not rescuing clumsy damsels in distress and jumping off bridges with an elastic rope tied to your ankles, where do you live?'

For the first time since she'd met him a shadow

shifted in the rich depths of his eyes before he blinked
and the resident twinkle was back.

'I'm based in London at the moment.'

She caught a hint of hesitancy, a slight stiffening
in his shoulders before his smile caught her off guard
again, dazzling in its sexiness.

'Boring financier job, huh? Lucky you quit.'

'Yeah, real lucky.'

She wanted to act blasé, as if she could walk out on
a solid job and live a carefree life traipsing around the
planet. Instead, she did what had been ingrained from
a young age: told the truth.

'Actually, I have no idea what I'm going to do next.'

'Easy. What's your dream job?'

His eyes crinkled in amusement, making her want to
smile along with him. Nothing fazed him. Then again,
the guy jumped off tall buildings for a living—losing
a job would be small fry.

'Dream job?'

She'd given up on dreams a long time ago, around
the time her life fell under the control of others.

'Yeah, what are you passionate about? Number
crunching in another capacity?'

'Hell no!'

He laughed at her vehemence. 'If not numbers, maybe
words? What about using your numbers experience and
using words to get your expertise across, maybe something like statistics lecturer or maths teacher?'

'Couldn't think of anything worse.'

Standing up in a room full of strangers watching her
every move? No way. Too reminiscent of her past.

He tapped his bottom lip, thinking, while she focused
on that lip. 'Words…hey, what about writing?'

Her heart skipped a beat at his suggestion. Writing

had once been a dream, a dream ripped asunder by the practicalities and expectations of being the prime minister's daughter. She hadn't written a word since Year Twelve English Lit, had turned her back on scrawling in her daily journals around the same time.

Ironically, when she'd been the brunt of the media's smear campaign recently she'd wish she could report the facts and not the drivel printed. It had sparked a vague idea about writing again, perhaps using her experience to freelance, to be an interviewer famed for her integrity rather than headline grabbing.

Maybe it'd be fun to try again, but could she make a living from it? And who would hire her, an ex-financier who'd been publicly flayed for no other crime than bearing the Beckett name?

'Take here, for instance, you'd have loads to write about.'

He snapped his fingers. 'Let's see. Melbourne's newest hip hotel has a resident poolside attendant that incapacitates guests then resuscitates them with a little mouth-to-mouth—'

'I kissed you,' she blurted, mortified when his gaze flicked to her lips before meeting hers again, filled with heat and longing that took her breath away.

'Yes, you did, and I can't tell you how impressed I am.'

Enjoying his lighthearted flirtation more than she could've imagined, she screwed up her eyes, pretending to think.

'With my technique? My impulsiveness? My—'

'All of it.'

This time his gaze started at her lips and swept over her and, while he couldn't see much beneath the voluminous grey robe, the smoulder told her he remembered every curve.

'You know I don't usually go around kissing strangers, right?'

'We're not strangers any more.'

He caressed her cheek, his finger starting at her temple and slowly stroking downwards towards her jaw, lingering under her chin to tip it up and when she looked into his eyes her temperature spiked.

Raw passion, the type of passion she'd read about in romance novels she'd hidden beneath her mattress as a teenager, a passion she secretly craved yet had never experienced, a passion she didn't believe in.

Until now.

For Roman didn't have to touch her to make her weak-kneed and hot. He didn't have to sweet-talk her or use lines or do anything other than look at her.

When those darker-than-chocolate eyes looked at her, *really* looked at her, every female cell in her body snapped to attention, a subliminal reaction she had no hope of controlling. Totally, irrationally crazy.

Increasingly flustered under his burning stare, she aimed for flippant.

'You should be safe from my randomly-lip-locking-strangers affliction, now we're properly introduced and all.'

'Pity.'

His thumb brushed her lower lip before his hand dropped away along with her belly and she floundered for a safe change of topic. There were only so many flirty comments and loaded stares a novice could handle.

'Are you here on business?'

'Of sorts.'

'Sounds cryptic.'

He shrugged, the action emphasising the tension in his shoulders. 'Time for new challenges so here I am.'

'Trying to find a higher mountain to jump off than the ones you've already conquered around the world?'

'Something like that.'

His smile didn't reach his eyes and she wondered why he was really here.

'What about you?'

'Me?'

'Are you up for new challenges? The writing idea?'

He'd subtly moved the focus back onto her. Interesting, as most of the guys in the social circles she'd moved in loved to talk about themselves but Roman seemed strangely reticent to discuss anything beyond here and now.

'Is it something you could go for?'

If he only knew. She'd loved writing as a kid, had penned her first full-blown dragon-and-princess fantasy at eight, had won a short story comp run by a Melbourne newspaper at eleven and got top marks in English every year at the private girls' school she'd attended.

Then her father had been elected Prime Minister and a starry-eyed fifteen year old with dreams of being a journalist-cum-fiction-writer had been indoctrinated into the expectations of a PM's daughter, sending her dreams along with the many vivid plots dancing in her mind straight down the toilet.

She'd followed a career path deemed more *suitable*, giving up her 'impulsive, flaky writing' to enter economics.

Oh, she'd done well, both at university and the merchant bank she'd worked for—not that she ever had an option for failure—but getting creative with figures wasn't a patch on getting creative with words and as her resentment had steadily built so had her frustration.

It had spilled over into all areas of her life, including her marriage, and while Leon had been amicable to the split she couldn't help but wonder if she'd been the major cause of the inevitable breakdown of their relationship.

'Yeah, writing for a living would be great.'

'What kind?'

'Probably freelance for a start.'

Give her a chance to free the muse and get the words flowing again, then see if anyone would truly employ her with zilch experience in the field.

'You should do it.'

Buoyed by his enthusiasm, she squared her shoulders. 'Maybe I will.'

'Good for you.'

He winked and her heart stuttered and stalled. 'Go ahead, paint a picture in words for me.'

'Now?'

'Yeah, no time like the present to get you started on your new career path.'

He leaned closer and she sucked in a breath of heady male tinged with chlorine. 'Describe your favourite holiday destination.'

'Lizard Island,' she blurted, needing to deflect those hypnotic dark eyes before she did something foolish, such as kiss him again. Though if her two-word answer was all she could come up with description-wise, she'd better ditch the writing idea now.

'Whitsunday Islands?'

She nodded. 'Not as well known as Hayman or Hamilton. Coastline's more rugged, beaches more isolated. Off the beaten track.'

'Unspoilt beauty can be more appealing than commercialised tourist traps.'

She silently chalked up another brownie point to him, in total agreement. She'd spent enough time traipsing around the world's hot spots with Leon: from Monte Carlo to New York, London to Tokyo, playing a diplomat's wife to perfection. Dining at Michelin-starred establishments, staying at exclusive spa resorts, mingling with the upper echelons of society, living the high life.

She would've rather camped in the Pyrenees and eaten hawker food and gone without pedicures than have her every move watched and scrutinised by people who almost wanted her to slip up so they could spread gossip or leak it to the press. Just as they had during her divorce.

She'd grown oblivious to the constant watching after a while, had pretended it hadn't bothered her, but it had taken its toll.

She'd spent the bulk of her life under a microscope and the fact that she was here, staying in a funky hotel under a pseudonym, flirting with an adventurous guy so far removed from the men in her social circle, was so freaking fantastic she wanted to shout it to the world.

Or do something crazy, something impulsive, something so far removed from her past to render her a new woman.

Grabbing his hand before she had second thoughts, she looked him straight in the eye.

'You know something? I'm pretty sure this concussion is worsening. Maybe you should walk me to my room after all?'

If he was surprised by her forwardness he didn't show it. A consummate performer. Then again, a guy who looked like him probably had women throwing themselves at him every day of the week. What was one more?

'Sure, no worries.'

He stood and held out a hand and as she stared at it she had a moment to change her mind.

Would she really go through with this? Invite a guy she barely knew back to her room? Have sex with him? Her first one-night stand?

'I'll just leave you at your door…'

His hand wavered but before he could lower it hers shot out and grabbed it as she surged to her feet, wobbly, off balance for a second before he steadied her.

She wanted to explain why she was doing this, wanted to give him a clue as to what this meant for her, but how to do it without sounding like a naïve moron?

'Ava, don't worry about it. If it's easier I'll leave you here—'

'I'm a prime minister's daughter and I'm four weeks out of a lacklustre marriage to a politician and I've spent my life doing the right thing and saying the right thing and I'm sick of it and I want a little adventure of my own and—'

'Shh…'

He placed a finger against her lips and she exhaled, embarrassed by her blurted admission.

Taking a deep breath to quell her mortification, she risked a quick glance at his face. If she saw pity, she was out of here.

Instead, his understanding had her swaying unconsciously towards him, her body recognising on some subconscious level what her mind only just realised.

This guy was special.

'You don't owe me any explanations.'

He lowered his finger, traced a path along her jaw,

under her ear, across her collarbone, lingering in the hollow there.

'I think you're amazing and if you want me to spend the night with you, the pleasure is all mine.'

Ava would've melted into a puddle of lust there and then if not for his strong arm sliding around her waist, supporting her as they strolled towards the lifts.

She didn't speak. She couldn't, not with her throat constricting and her diaphragm heaving and her pulse pounding so hard she could barely hear herself think.

When they reached the lifts he squeezed her gently and she automatically snuggled into his side.

'You sure about this?'

She hadn't been sure about taking an economics major, she hadn't been sure about marrying Leon and she sure as hell wasn't sure what she'd do next career-wise but if there was one thing she was sure of tonight this was it.

'Does room 1620 answer your question?'

She held her breath as he guided her into the elevator, hit the sixteen button and brushed a soft kiss across her lips.

'Perfectly,' he said as they stood like silent sentinels, watching the panel counting down the numbers from twenty-seven to sixteen, and when the elevator pinged and the doors slid open on the sixteenth floor she could've sworn she experienced an adrenalin rush no jump off a bridge could ever hope to reproduce.

CHAPTER THREE

ROMAN had exactly sixty seconds to extricate himself from this situation and make a run for it.

How many times had he aborted a jump due to risky conditions? Or rescheduled a climb for another day due to changeable, unfavourable winds?

Too many to count and right now he had that same churning in his gut telling him something wasn't right.

He knew what it was. Despite her forwardness Ava had vulnerable written all over her. And he'd had a gutful of susceptible females, considering the major reason he'd fled to Australia was to get as far away from one as possible.

Not entirely fair, as Ava had more strength in her little finger than Estelle had in her entire passive-aggressive body, but fresh from another emotionally draining bout with his moody mother left him with little impetus to fall headlong into another potentially fragile situation, even if it was for only a night.

Ava practically bounced along beside him as they traversed the long corridor to her room, oblivious to his dilemma.

For that was what he was facing: lose himself for a night in a wild, passionate encounter guaranteed to refresh or give the woman beside him another reason to doubt herself if he ditched her at her door.

She'd do it too, probably rehash their pool encounter at length and come to the erroneous conclusion that she'd said or done something wrong to drive him away.

He'd hate that, for he could see she'd already had the life squished out of her. Being a prime minister's daughter would've been hell, not to mention a politician's wife, and the fact she'd gathered enough courage to invite him back to her room for a one-night stand spoke volumes.

A month out of a divorce, she needed to test the freedom waters. It had nothing to do with getting laid and everything to do with asserting a femininity he'd hazard a guess had been battered.

He'd seen mates go through divorces and one word summed them up. Ugly. How much harder had it been for Ava, with the added pressure of her family name?

The right thing to do would be to walk her to her door, kiss her goodnight and wish her a happy life. The last thing she needed was a guy who made an art out of escapism, who'd outrun an Olympian at the first sign of anything deeper than casual.

And Ava needed *deeper*. She needed a good guy to nurse her through this tender period, a guy to build her confidence, a guy to be there for her.

He sure as hell wasn't that guy.

He'd make sure she made it safely back to her room, try to assure her he'd had a fun evening and make a run for it.

Decision made, he risked a sideways glance at her, his gut instantly tightening and making a mockery of his resolution.

Water droplets clung to the strands of hair framing

her glowing face, her skin still dewy and damp from their pool encounter. Her body was completely covered in the hotel's voluminous robe but he could remember every intriguing detail: the nip of her waist, the flare of her hips, her smooth caramel-toned legs, her breasts...

The tension within him coiled tighter, strangling his resolve to leave her and walk away. He knew what he had to do. Shame his libido wasn't with the programme yet.

'Almost there.'

A barely detectable tremor underscored her husky tone and in that second his intention to leave her alone took a serious hit.

Her susceptibility was the one thing driving him away yet that audible hint of vulnerability had him wanting to hold her close all night.

He wasn't usually a sucker for a damsel in distress—discounting Estelle, who'd worked out he was an easy target for a single mother and who never let him forget that fact every day of his life.

Nope, he usually went for confident, showy women. Women proud of their assets, who knew how to use them. Women like him. Nothing wrong with grabbing the spotlight and staying there, something he'd perfected out of necessity.

So why was he so hung up over a naive divorcee primed to test her newfound independence?

'Here we are.'

With her back to the door, she gazed at him with a gut-punching mix of wary optimism and expected rejection. The rejection hit him hardest, as if she'd expected him to walk away all along.

'You sure—'

Her fingertips pressed against his lips, effectively

silencing him, and when her hand trailed slowly downwards, her palm coming to rest over his heart, he knew he couldn't do it.

Walking away would be like kicking a defenceless puppy. Not that he pitied her, far from it. He admired her pluck in a world that must be topsy-turvy for her right about now.

Women reeling from divorces might want to assert their independence but often didn't follow through so the fact they'd got this far notched up his admiration further.

When her palm slid lower, lingered on his upper abs, her fingers tentatively exploring, he didn't pity her or admire her, he just plain wanted her and taking a step closer, their bodies barely touching, he knew that whatever happened when they stepped through that door, he wanted to make this night memorable for her.

When Ava had headed for a late-night swim she hadn't expected to bring back a visitor to her room so when she slid the key card into the slot and opened the door to her room, she baulked.

'Problem?'

Yeah, there was a problem.

She'd never done this before.

Inviting a guy she'd just met back to her room for sex? So far out of the realms of reality to be ludicrous. Except for the fact she had an incredibly hot, amazingly gorgeous guy hovering behind her, waiting for them to take their flirtation all the way.

Was she nervous? Hell yeah, but anticipation far outweighed her nerves.

A moment ago, she'd thought Roman would kiss her

goodnight and walk away. He'd had that look, the look of a guy wanting to do the right thing.

She never should've blurted that stuff about being recently divorced; for all she knew, this was a pity lay.

Would it matter? Considering how Roman had made her feel the last hour, probably not. She wanted to explore the attraction between them, wanted to see if the excitement making her nerves buzz and her muscles clench could carry over into the best sex of her life.

Staying in this hotel had been all about a fresh start and what better way to kick-start her new life than with an unforgettable night with a guy who made her insides quiver with a single look?

A delicious shiver ran through her as Roman nuzzled her ear, his arms sliding around her waist from behind, pulling her close to reveal evidence of how he could make all her problems vanish over the next few hours.

'The place is a mess,' she said, tilting her head back to look at him.

'I'm not here to check out the place.'

His mouth crushed hers in a breath-stealing kiss to prove it and her last-minute doubts faded into oblivion.

When he finally gave her a chance to breathe again, she said, 'Right, now we've cleared that up, come on in.'

Laughing, they tumbled through the door and as it slammed shut they reached for each other, oblivious to the mess, oblivious to everything but satisfying the hunger that had started with an unexpected kiss.

Ava wanted to tear off his robe, push him against the nearest wall and jump him.

She settled for tugging on his robe sash so hard he slammed against her and she staggered slightly, getting her wish reversed when her back hit the wall.

'Uh…it's been a while for me,' she said, feeling the need to explain her desperate behaviour.

In response he captured her face between his hands and kissed her, long, hot, open-mouthed kisses that made further explanations unnecessary.

Her knees would've buckled if he hadn't pressed his body to hers, holding her upright with every delicious, hard plane.

As his tongue danced with hers she strummed his shoulders, his back, revelling in the defined muscles, the lean sinews.

When her hands moved lower, exploring the contours of one very fine ass, he moaned, pressing his pelvis into hers, making her crumple just that little bit more.

'You're driving me wild,' he murmured against the side of her mouth and she groped him, unable to keep the smug grin off her face.

She'd never driven any guy wild in her entire life and to think a guy like Roman, who'd probably had enough adrenalin rushes to keep him high for life, found her exciting enough to drive him wild…well, it was the best aphrodisiac ever.

'You think this is funny?'

'I think this is fantastic,' she said, her fingertips toying with the waist of his wet board shorts.

The corner of his mouth kicked up along with an eyebrow.

'Then why the grin?'

'Because I'm happier than I've been in a while.'

The truth spilled out and as surprise lit his eyes she wished she could take it back.

This wasn't the time for stark reality.

This was a time to forget the past; to live in the future.

Before he could ask any more questions or she could blurt out any more mood-killers, she wrapped a leg around him, surprised when he murmured, 'Me too,' in her ear.

Before she could ponder why a rich, gorgeous, adventurous guy like him would be anything other than happy he systematically ravaged her, starting at the top and working his way down.

He ripped off her robe and her nipples instantly hardened as he stared at her breasts through the wet Lycra.

Her simple navy one-piece was conservative by swimsuit standards these days but the way Roman devoured her with his eyes made her feel as if she wore the skimpiest, sexiest swimsuit ever.

Not that she was wearing it for long.

Hooking his thumbs under the straps, he peeled them down.

Slowly.

Revealing one breast first, then another, his hungry stare making her skin pebble.

She sucked in a breath as he continued stripping her, kneeling in front of her as he tugged the swimsuit lower…and lower…his breath fanning her belly.

Lower still and she stiffened as the swimsuit snagged on her butt. Using his hands, he slid them under the Lycra and eased it over and down her legs, baring her to him and she shivered, more from the intensity and hunger in his stare than the air-conditioned chill in the air.

'Jeez,' he murmured, his hands stroking her ankles, her calves, the backs of her knees, lingering on the insides of her thighs and gently nudging her apart.

She watched him, so turned on she couldn't think,

couldn't breathe, for wanting him to touch the part of her throbbing for him.

Second after torturous second passed before his head eased forward and his mouth finally touched her where she yearned to be touched.

Her pelvis arched as his tongue flicked her, once, twice and she whimpered, the tension within her spiralling out of control too soon, too fast.

But she was powerless to stop it and as he spread her further, his tongue lapping at her, she came apart on a drawn-out scream.

Senseless, boneless, she would've slid down the wall if his strong hands hadn't braced her waist and as he kissed his way upwards, his tongue tracing a slow, scorching path towards her breasts, her need for him increased.

'That was…ooh…'

His mouth clamped around a nipple, sucking it while his hand kneaded her other breast, and the tension started again, coiling, tightening.

She wanted to say that was spectacular, sensational, stupendous, and a whole host of other totally inadequate adjectives. But he didn't give her time to think.

Before shrugging off his robe he pulled his wallet out of the pocket, snaffled a foil packet, stripped off his board shorts as if it were the most natural thing in the world and made quick work of a condom.

While she struggled to breathe as she watched the entire time.

Time slowed as she watched him roll the condom over his arousal, thick and long, and she clenched her hands to stop from reaching out and finishing the job for him.

When she finally wrenched her gaze away, she

sucked in a breath, for he was looking at her the same way: wide-eyed, dazed and ravenous.

Needing him inside her, now, she opened her arms to him and he didn't need to be asked twice.

His hands splayed her waist as he hoisted her up and she wrapped her legs around him.

He nudged her entrance and she moaned as he slid in, inch by exquisite inch, until he filled her.

His mouth claimed hers as he started to move, gliding in and out, trying to keep it slow.

But she didn't want slow. She wanted hard and fast. She wanted the type of sex she'd never had.

Her pelvis took on a life of its own as she bucked against him, urging him on and he obliged, pumping into her until she was mindless, clawing to the edge of another monumental orgasm before falling over the other side in a blaze of heat and glory.

He came a second later, thrusting up so high she almost passed out with pleasure and as they clung to each other, sweat-slicked skin gleaming in the lamplight, she couldn't help but wish she'd been this adventurous a long time ago.

CHAPTER FOUR

Ava had no idea about morning-after etiquette. How could she, when the only guy she'd ever slept with had been Leon and they'd been dating for ever before they'd finally had sex?

There'd been no awkward mulling over what to say or when to leave or how to extricate herself gracefully from the situation then, for they'd practically been engaged anyway. They'd known each other so long, as family friends first, later as a couple, that sleeping together had been no big deal.

Unlike now.

Roman slid into his hotel bathrobe and belted it, looking as delectably sexy as he did without it.

His hair spiked every which way, he had some serious stubble going on and the faintest dark circles under his eyes indicating he hadn't slept much.

Snap, neither had she.

She wasn't complaining.

Trying not to cower under the sheets like the one-night-stand novice she was, she scooted up the bed, semi-sitting as he stalked towards her, aiming for post-coital cool when in fact she probably had bed hair and morning breath.

Sitting on the edge of the bed, he took hold of her

hand and kissed the back of it, a grand romantic gesture that merely added to the surrealism of their encounter.

'I have to go. Meeting.'

'No worries, I've got stuff to do too.'

And if she didn't get him out of here so she could shower and get her head screwed on right she'd make a mess of this.

Roman had been a lovely distraction, an incredible, mind-blowing distraction, but she needed to refocus on getting the rest of her life back on track and the faster they made a clean break, the better.

Gently extricating her hand out of his, she touched his cheek, the stubble rasping deliciously against her fingertips.

'Last night was...'

What? The most exciting night of her life? The best sex she'd ever had? The most spontaneous, adventurous, outrageous thing she'd ever done?

She wanted to thank him, to explain what last night had meant to her—shedding her old life, welcoming her new—but one glance at his face and she knew she couldn't say any of those things.

For Roman had reverted to the suave charmer she'd first met last night, the guy whose lips quirked as if he found everything amusing, the guy whose eyes crinkled in the corners from laughing a lot, the guy who lived life on the edge and wouldn't understand how monumental last night had been to a staid, regular girl like her.

Smiling, he cradled her face in his hands. 'I think this sums up what last night was.'

His kiss was slow, sensual and steeped in eroticism. A kiss to remind her of what they'd shared; a kiss to ensure she'd never forget.

When their lips eased apart all too soon her fingers convulsed against the sheets to stop from reaching out and hauling him back for more.

'Thanks, Roman.'

The second the words popped out she felt stupid. Did you thank a guy for sex? For the hottest night of your life? She had no idea of rules in this situation and for a girl who'd followed protocols her entire life she didn't like this floundering.

'My pleasure.'

He touched her shoulder once before standing, the few centimetres separating them feeling like an ocean already.

Last night had been about sex.

Last night had been about sizzle.

Then why the crazy, irrational ache in her chest as she watched him stroll towards the door? For a moment she wanted to run after him, grab hold of that robe and rip it off as she had last night.

Biting her bottom lip to stop from saying anything else, she pasted a bright smile on her face as he stopped at the door and turned back.

'If you have any free time, I'm staying another day.'

Unsure whether he wanted to see her again or was reverting to type with the flirtation, she managed a mute nod and some stupid half-salute as he let himself out.

The minute the door closed, she slumped down the bed and flung her forearm over her eyes.

Maybe that would block out the stupid voice in her head, the one that insisted she had the guts to discover his room number and ring him before he left.

Ludicrous, as one-night stands were just that: one night.

But in the time it took to reject the idea as ridiculous,

frivolous and totally unreal, she had envisioned herself having dinner, a midnight swim and possibly a whole lot more with the guy who had rocked her world.

Roman glanced at his watch as he entered the Michelin-starred restaurant on the hotel's ground floor. He was running late. Not that he cared. The cause of his tardiness had been worth it.

And how.

Even now, forty-five minutes later, he couldn't get the last image of Ava out of his head. Tousled, wide-eyed, sated, sitting up in bed clutching a sheet to hide what he'd already seen and admired and tasted all night long.

She'd looked so vulnerable, the exact opposite of the wild, passionate woman she'd been in his arms, and it had taken every ounce of will power to walk away from her.

Though what would hanging around have achieved? They'd had a memorable one-night stand. They had separate lives to lead on different continents. They had nothing in common beyond what they'd shared last night.

So why that parting shot about how long he was staying here? The last thing he needed was a newly divorced woman finding her feet in singledom latching onto him.

He mentally winced at that poor judgement call. Nothing Ava had said or done implied she'd be latching onto anyone any time soon. In fact, from what she'd said, she'd spent her life under a microscope and was probably looking for a little freedom.

Being the prime minister's daughter would've sucked. As for her marriage to a politician, he'd schmoozed with enough A-listers around the world to know how these things worked. Family expectations, moving in the right social circles, marrying a partner deemed suitable.

He'd bet his last grappling hook Ava had said all the right things and done all the right things from birth, had probably married some slick politician hand-picked by Daddy. Poor kid.

Then again, her inherent naivety had attracted him right from the beginning. She'd seemed oblivious to their physical proximity when he'd rescued her after their heads collided but he'd been all too aware of her slick body millimetres from his.

She'd been flustered; he'd been aroused.

Then he'd started flirting and while she'd reciprocated there'd been an innocence about her, an inexperience that didn't gel with a divorcee. In his travels, how many times did he meet a woman who still blushed? Not often.

He dated extensively, from princesses to pop starlets, blondes, brunettes and every shade in between. Not that he was half the playboy the paparazzi made him out to be but he was a well-known, successful, single guy and that status came with perks. Plenty of perks.

So what was it about Ava that shook him up?

Once he'd left her room he should've forgotten about her, should've focused on this meeting. Instead, he wondered how soon he could wrap up business and maybe ring her, see if she was free for a quick catch-up before they both went their separate ways.

Rattled more than he cared to admit, he tugged on the ends of his shirt sleeves and adjusted his cufflinks, the same steadying ritual he went through before any jump. Though in his sporting career it was usually a buckle or safety knot he was adjusting.

Glancing around the restaurant, he spotted Rex Mayfair, an old friend of his mum's, partially hidden by a screen and towering palm.

Rex had often stopped by their Chelsea apartment when he'd visited London and as a kid he'd wondered if Rex might in fact be his dad. Despite careful scrutiny, it didn't look as if the old guy was anything more than a platonic friend of Estelle's. Not that she'd tell him anyway. He'd given up asking about his paternity years ago.

'Father unknown' sucked on his birth certificate but not as much as having a mother who'd made him pay for being a burr in her side every day growing up.

Annoyed he'd let old bitterness creep into this otherwise sensational morning, he strode across the restaurant, ready to hear what Rex thought of his plan.

Rex caught sight of him first and stood, a welcoming smile accentuating the many creases lining his ruddy face.

'Roman, my boy, good to see you.'

'Likewise.'

As he neared the table and reached out to shake Rex's hand a prickle of awareness raised his hackles and he glanced over his shoulder to find Ava sitting at the next table, partially hidden by a palm, poring over the morning newspaper's employment section.

The smart thing to do would be to acknowledge her with a greeting then distance himself and catch up with Rex. Easy. Until he caught sight of her teeth worrying her lower lip and the frantic eye movements speed-reading the job ads.

She needed a break and as Rex pumped his hand an idea completely out of left-field smacked him upside the head.

'Excuse me a moment.'

Rex raised an eyebrow as Roman squatted next to Ava's chair.

'We meet again.'

Her head snapped up, her blue eyes wide with panic until she registered who it was. 'Hey there.'

They lapsed into an awkward silence and he stood, touching her lightly on the back. 'If you're free, I'd like you to meet someone.'

Confusion creased her brow but she wouldn't refuse; etiquette training would be hard to shake.

'Sure.'

She stood, her arm brushing his and he gritted his teeth against the urge to touch her.

He should've done the right thing and walked away last night but he hadn't been able to conquer his insatiable hunger for her. Now he had a chance to make things right, to take her vulnerability and turn it into the confidence of a young woman revelling in a fresh start.

'Rex, I'd like you to meet Ava, a friend of mine.'

She shot him a dubious look at his mention of friend, which he ignored and gestured to the seat between Rex and his.

'Pleased to meet you, young lady.'

'Likewise.'

Before Rex's journalistic instincts kicked in and he prodded Ava for info on how they met, he angled his body towards her.

'Rex is the chief editor of *Globetrotter* magazine.'

A spark lit her eyes, quickly replaced by suspicion. Clever girl—he knew she'd cotton on to the rationale behind this introduction.

'Must be an interesting job.'

Oblivious to the simmering tension, Rex waxed lyrical about his work while Roman relaxed into his chair, very much aware of the freshly showered, floral-scented woman beside him.

How could he not be, when every cell in his body screamed for a repeat of what they'd done last night?

All night.

That scent…a rich, evocative blend…rose and lilacs she'd told him, a fragrance imprinted on his receptors, a fragrance to drive a man wild.

He straightened, needing to get to the crux of this meeting so he could flee before he did something crazy, such as drag her back to his room and throw away the key.

'Rex, last time we spoke you mentioned expanding the layout for *Globetrotter*? Starting to incorporate human interest interviews, that kind of thing?'

Rex folded his hands and leaned on the table. 'I know that's why you're here, trying to get that mug of yours into my magazine.'

Roman chuckled. 'That too. Though maybe I can do you a favour in return?'

'What's that?'

'Ava's a writer. If you're looking for new slots to fill, she's your gal.'

Ava blanched and he rushed on. 'You've got mainly freelancers on staff, right? She'd be a huge asset to the magazine.'

He could practically hear her teeth grinding behind the practised smile she gave Rex, while she reserved a death glare for him.

He grinned in response, draping an arm across the back of her chair and murmuring, 'You can thank me later.'

She kicked him under the table.

'Most of our freelancers are snowed under so I was looking at putting new people on...' Rex narrowed his eyes, assessing. 'You interested, Ava? You could do a piece for me, shoot it across, I'll take a look and let you know if we have ongoing assignments for you? Sound doable?'

Ava's fingers pleated the tablecloth while she nodded, her eyes sparkling with an enthusiasm that hit him like a wayward waterski to the chest.

'Sounds great, thanks for the opportunity.'

Rex steepled his fingers, his shrewd gaze flicking between the two of them. 'In fact, I think I can kill two birds with the proverbial stone. My buddy Roman here was trying to take advantage of our long-standing friendship and grab a profile spot in the revamped *Globetrotter*. Why don't you do your piece on him? Kind of like an exposé on extreme sports, focusing on the personal angle.'

Ah...this just got better and better.

'I'm game.'

This time he avoided her kick in time.

The epitome of a poised pro, Ava clasped her hands together and nodded. 'Thanks, Rex, I'll get straight on it.'

'Better pack your bags, then.'

The heat from her narrowed eyes could've melted him. 'Why's that?'

'Change of plans. I'm leaving for Surfers Paradise today.'

By the mutinous twist of her lips she didn't want to fly to Queensland with him. Wait 'til she heard about the private jet.

'If it's okay with you I'll arrange another room at the hotel I'm staying at?'

Her wary gaze clashed with his and it sent an unexpected jolt through him, catapulting him straight back to last night and the same hesitancy she'd shown when their flirting hotted up.

He'd seen the conflicting emotions flicker across her face then—caution, mistrust, yearning, excitement—and as she met his gaze now, unflinching, he saw the same myriad emotions.

He knew the moment she made a decision, for a determined glitter replaced previous chariness.

'Fine by me.'

Her bright smile managed to encompass him and Rex at the same time. 'When do we leave?'

'That's the spirit.' Rex rubbed his hands together as if he'd masterminded a huge deal. 'How about we make the deadline a week from today?'

'Sounds good. I'll email you my details.'

When Rex stood Ava held out her hand and Roman noticed the jagged edges of her cuticles where she'd been picking at them beneath the table.

Doubt wasn't in his vocabulary but at that moment he wondered if he'd done the right thing, shoving her in Rex's face, almost insisting Rex hire her so the old guy had no option but to make an offer out of politeness.

Considering the sideways glares she kept shooting him, he'd soon find out.

Rex shook Ava's hand. 'Look forward to seeing what you can do.'

Ava visibly straightened and glowed under the faith Rex showed in her, making Roman wonder if she'd received much of it growing up. Had she been ignored by her father, too busy running the country to bestow attention on his kid? Had she been raised by nannies? Did she have any siblings?

He never wondered about women he'd slept with, content to keep his liaisons short and sweet. So what was it about this one that raised a heap of questions he wanted answers to?

'As for you, you'll have your spot in *Globetrotter*. And say hi to your mother when you see her.'

Rex slapped him on the back and he bit back a grin when Ava frowned. Curiosity about his relationship with Rex was probably burning her up.

He could string it out, make her ask, but he'd be pushing his luck. He'd gained enough ground having her agree to accompany him, especially considering last night. Best to smooth the way for he had a feeling they'd be seeing a lot more of each other over the next few days.

He waited while Rex wound his way between tables before turning back to Ava. Before he could explain, she braced forearms on the table and leaned forward.

'Did you plan this?'

Gone was the wide-eyed ingénue. In her place was a narrow-eyed less-than-impressed woman.

'When? Last night?'

A faint pink stained her cheeks, making her blue eyes sparkle with fire. 'Yeah, then. This morning. Before now.'

Knowing it would drive her crazy, he reached across and patted her hand. She didn't disappoint, visibly recoiling from his patronisation.

'Rex is an old family friend. I'm after more exposure for a new sport so he met me here to tee it up.'

'You still haven't answered my question.'

She hadn't budged an inch and he admired her all the more.

'No, I didn't *plan* this.'

He waved his hands between them. 'It didn't click 'til I walked in here, saw you scanning the job ads and remembered what we discussed last night about dream jobs.'

'But I'm not a writer!'

'You will be if you treat me gently, use your most persuasive interview techniques and compose a killer article.'

'You're a pain in the—'

'You can thank me later,' he said, clasping his hands behind his head and leaning back, enjoying their banter as much as he'd enjoyed having his hands all over her last night. Well, maybe not as much as that.

'Thanks,' she muttered begrudgingly, crossing her arms and leaning on the table. 'But did you stop to think if I mess this up...?'

Her fingers fidgeted with the cutlery and, stung by a pang of remorse, he straightened. He recognised the fear in her eyes, experienced a fleeting flash of it every time he stood on top of a cliff or had his toes curled around the edge of an open plane door.

The fear of stuffing up and facing the consequences. And while Ava's weren't life and death, for someone as fragile as her at the moment, on the crest of starting a new life, failing at this would terrify her.

He touched her hand, stilled it. 'If you mess up, you start over at something else. If writing is your passion, you deserve to give it a go.'

The corners of her mouth curled slightly. 'I'm still mad at you for interfering like that.'

'Promise not to do it again.' He held up two fingers to his temple. 'Scout's honour.'

'Something tells me you were never in Scouts.'

Glad they'd moved onto safer ground, flirtatious ground, a ground he understood well, he sat back and clasped his hands behind his head.

'Not angelic enough?'

Her gaze momentarily dipped to his lips, as if remembering exactly how non-angelic he could be.

'You really want me to answer that?'

Enjoying their sparring, surprised by how easily it turned him on, he grinned.

'Please do.'

Darting a quick glance around them to ensure no one was eavesdropping, she shifted her chair a little closer to his and his libido kicked into overdrive.

'Angels have wings and halos.' She pointed to the top of his head. 'You, on the other hand, have horns.'

'How do you figure?'

'That collision in the pool? The bump on my head?'

A coy little smile tilted her mouth and tilted his world off its axis.

'Definitely the result of coming into contact with the devil.'

He laughed outright. 'Don't forget my tail.'

She blushed again and, unable to resist, he trailed a fingertip down her cheek.

'I was referring to the fact it may be pointy to go with the horns, but if you were thinking of something else…'

'You know damn well you're much better at this flirting stuff than me.'

She swatted his hand away like an annoying fly.

'Think we established that among other things last night.'

She didn't sound uneasy but he noticed her hands had resumed their nervous plucking, pleating a linen serviette this time.

'Is that why you're uptight? The fact we'll be travelling to the Gold Coast together?'

'And the rest,' she muttered, finding her serviette pleating infinitely more interesting than looking at him.

She meant the hotel. His libido had roared the instant she'd agreed to stay, separate rooms or not.

'I'm a big boy and the Palazzo is a big hotel. If you don't want to see me when we're not working, I'm sure the place is big enough for the both of us.'

Her eyebrows shot up. 'We're staying at the Palazzo Versace?'

'That's right, six star all the way.'

Eager to tease another smile out of her, he added, 'Stick with me, kid, and I'll take you places.'

Thankfully, her lips eased into a smile. 'The hotel's not the problem.'

'Then what is?'

After a lengthy pause, she finally glanced up and the apprehensive fervour in her glowing blue eyes kicked him where he wanted to feel it least: his chest.

'How I'll do the best job possible on an article I need to nail while being distracted by the guy who rocked my world last night.'

Speechless at her honesty, he grabbed her hand, surprised yet pleased when she didn't yank it away.

Defiant, she tossed her shoulder-length blonde hair in a gesture he hazarded a guess she'd never done in her life.

'What? Nothing to say? That's gotta be a first for you.'

Aroused beyond belief by her beguiling contrasts, shy to bravado in a blink, he eased into a grin.

'Do you have any idea how hot you are when you're all riled up?'

She rolled her eyes, but not before he'd glimpsed a pleased smile hovering at the corners of her mouth.

'Yeah, that's me, a regular Angelina Jolie.'

Raising her hand to his lips, he brushed a kiss across the back, buoyed by her sharp intake.

'Sweetheart, you're way hotter than any movie star.'

'Now I know you're full of it,' she said, but she still didn't slide her hand from his.

'Full of admiration for you.'

She screwed up her nose. 'That's a woeful line.'

Jeez, he loved her quick-fire responses. 'Well, I guess if you don't believe that, you won't believe the rest.'

A brow raised in a perfectly inverted comma. 'The rest?'

'Could be fate we're staying together at a luxurious hotel hot on the heels of what happened last night?'

'Rubbish,' she muttered, tempering her blunt opinion with a demure smile. 'Don't believe in fate.'

'What do you believe in?'

She pondered the question, shadows clouding her eyes, and the fact she had to think about her answer spoke volumes.

If he'd been asked what he believed in he could respond instantly: the mind-clearing clarity that came the moment before a B.A.S.E. jump, the peaks of the world's tallest mountains, the guaranteed adrenalin rush of a free fall.

Solid, dependable things he'd come to rely on, things that didn't let him down, things that didn't use him when convenient then throw him away like a ripped parachute.

He'd almost given up on a response when she finally cleared her throat.

'My writing—I believe in that.'

'Good to hear.'

She gnawed on a deliciously full bottom lip, something he'd done repeatedly last night. 'I can't believe I'm actually doing this. I always loved it but did an economics degree at uni, ended up working for a major international bank instead.'

Bitterness mingled with regret rolled off her and a smart guy would leave well enough alone. But he didn't usually have these deep conversations with women and the fact she trusted him enough to reveal some inner secret made him feel ten feet tall.

'Why?'

She looked unbearably cute as she wrinkled her nose. 'Apparently writing is a "frivolous, unstable occupation". End quote.'

He winced. 'Your dad?'

'Yeah. Guess the prime minister's daughter needed to have an upstanding, reputable career in economics rather than freelance writing, or worse.'

She lowered her voice and crooked her finger at him. 'Maybe even penning a fiction novel? The scandal!'

'You should do it, you know. Write a novel.'

He snapped his fingers. 'Not just any novel. A juicy romance novel. A saga spanning generations with loads of scandal and a pompous prime minister who gets his comeuppance in the end.'

She smiled and he warmed to his topic. 'Or better yet, if we're talking scandalising your family, why not go the whole hog and pen steamy erotica?'

Her eyebrows shot up as he tapped his lip and pretended to think before his hand shot out and captured hers.

'I can help.'

His thumb caressed her pulse point, his own pulse rampaging when her tongue darted out to moisten her lip.

'How about I assist with the extensive research you'd have to do?'

He brought her hand to his mouth and nibbled on the pad of her thumb, savouring her reaction: the slight tremor of her arm, the sway towards him, the wistful sigh.

'For authenticity's sake.'

His lips trailed to the inside of her wrist and his tongue swirled, making her gasp.

'Because we know every good author does thorough research, right?'

Her eyes widened to fathomless blue pools as he slowly unfurled her fingers one by one, exposing her palm, before planting a lingering kiss there.

'What do you say?'

Dragging in a deep breath, she eased her hand from his, but not before he'd seen a glimmer of reluctance.

'Thanks for the offer but I think I'll try and master freelance writing before moving on to unfamiliar territory.'

It was his turn to be shocked. She'd been married and by her passionate responses to the wild sex last night he doubted that territory was all that unfamiliar.

Belatedly realising her faux pas, she opened her mouth, snapped it shut, before the flash of determination in her eyes alerted him to another incoming revelation.

'Bet you think I'm tragic, huh? Being married for two years and still finding…you know…sex…unfamiliar.'

'Not tragic, but I'm confused.'

She glanced away, embarrassed, and he wished he'd left well enough alone. She'd been responding to his flirting, hadn't pulled away, now this.

'Look, you don't owe me any explanations—'

Her gaze clashed with his, suddenly fierce. 'Last night? My first one-night stand. Protected upbringing, dating a family friend for years before doing the right thing and marrying him, discovering that good friends doesn't equal fireworks in the bedroom…well, you get the picture.'

She grimaced and pity clawed at him. Pity she wouldn't appreciate if that steely gleam in her eyes was any indication.

'And yes, if you do the math, I've now been with two guys in my lifetime. Sad case, huh?'

Hating her slumped shoulders, her down-turned mouth, he gripped her shoulders and leaned close enough so they were inches apart.

'Listen up, sweetheart, cos I'm only going to say this once. It's the quality not the quantity that matters and speaking from personal experience last night you blew my mind.'

A corner of her mouth kicked up and his unimpressionable heart went twang again. 'Really?'

'Hell yeah.'

Pulling her close, he murmured in her ear, 'The kind of explosive sex we had last night? Not so common.'

He nibbled her ear lobe.

'You—' He sucked the lobe into his mouth.

'Were—' He tongued it.

'Freaking—' His mouth drifted south, to the tender skin under her ear, where he nipped.

'Amazing.'

He didn't have to move as her lips sought his, as frantic, as needy, as exquisite as last night's first kiss, the tension simmering between them reigniting in a blaze of unquenchable heat.

His mind blanked for long, endless seconds until he realised where they were. In a famous chef's restaurant that might just have paparazzi lurking around and he'd be damned if he scared Ava off before they got a chance to really create some major fireworks.

His lips eased, lingered a few exquisite moments before he pulled back and tipped up her chin with a fingertip.

'I have a question for you.'

She blinked; it did little to erase the stunned shock in the aftermath of their cataclysmic kiss.

'What?'

'Care to continue this somewhere more private?' He screwed up his eyes, pretending to think. 'Like some swish suite at the Palazzo Versace over the next few days?'

He expected her to baulk.

He expected her to backtrack.

He expected her to distance herself and throw out a host of plausible excuses and allow logic to override passion.

What he didn't expect was the dazzling smile that made him want to sweep her into his arms and hightail it out of here before he kissed her again.

'If you're asking me to indulge in a wild, no-holds-barred, impulsive fling over the next few days?'

She beckoned him closer and this time her breath tickled his ear, her lips brushing it and sending a shudder of desire through him.

'My answer's hell yes.'

CHAPTER FIVE

Ava had flown on private jets many times. They didn't impress her any more than the jet's occupants who usually bored her to death with shop talk: political analysis, evaluation of the world's economy, muck-raking opponents in the next election.

Yet the moment she stepped onto this jet and saw Roman reclining against a cream leather lounge, laughing at something the steward had said, she knew this flight would be very different from others.

As she studied his laid-back posture, one arm casually draped across the back of the lounge, his ivory business shirt unbuttoned, the amethyst tie he'd been wearing earlier peeping out of his jacket where he'd slung it over the back of a nearby chair, one ankle resting on the opposite knee, she saw a man comfortable in his surroundings, a man used to the finer things in life, a man not averse to flying in private jets.

Which begged the question: who *was* this guy?

She'd been attracted to him right from the start because of his adventurous streak, the extreme sports guy as alien to her world as the thought of jumping off a building with a parachute strapped to her back.

Sure, Roman was hot and had a body finely honed through many hours of insane leaping off things, but it had been that underlying recklessness that had set her blood boiling, the hint of daredevil that had encouraged her to shuck off every ingrained reservation she'd grown up with and gone for it.

Last night had been memorable but she'd been reluctantly ready to push it from her mind; until he strode into the restaurant this morning and arranged her life.

She couldn't believe he'd done that, practically foisting her onto Rex Mayfair, taking advantage of their friendship, giving the guy no option but to hire her.

At the time she'd inwardly seethed, hating his take-charge attitude. She'd spent enough of her life falling in with arrangements to loathe the slightest hint of bossiness now but considering the result…

She had a chance at gaining employment in a field she loved. Much quicker than she could've anticipated and much easier than padding a CV with her out-of-date writing skills, going through countless interviews only to be told she didn't have enough experience.

Roman's interference rankled but she couldn't hold it against him, especially considering the future of her new career rested on him.

Of all the people she had to interview, it had to be him.

A guy she knew in *intimate* detail, from the ragged scar low on his right hip from a skiing accident to the tiny chunk of missing left bicep gouged by a jagged rock while abseiling.

And the rest…

She tried not to squirm at the memory of *the rest*, knowing she'd have to focus on the facts to nail this. Solid interview questions, neat prose and effective editing would get the job done.

It was what would happen *after* the working day ended that had her tied in knots.

How had she gone from quietly celebrating her new-found freedom away from the paparazzi's prying eyes to having a one-night stand with an adventurer and getting a job out of it?

Seeing him so soon after their unforgettable, erotic encounter, wearing a designer suit as opposed to a hotel bathrobe, had thrown her this morning. Next thing she knew she'd been offered a job that included travelling with a hot guy on a jet to a swanky hotel.

But you chose to take it further, accepting his offer for a fling.

Staring at Roman, with his impressive tan and dark wavy hair slicked to perfection and decadent chocolate eyes, she couldn't blame herself.

Any red-blooded, recently divorced, single woman who'd lived like an automaton would've grabbed this opportunity with both hands. Hands that had willingly and wantonly travelled over every inch of his incredibly toned, incredibly sexy body and were itching for more.

He glanced up at that moment and she swallowed to ease the tightness of her throat. Hoping her face didn't betray the turn her thoughts had taken, she raised a hand in a casual wave.

He smiled and her throat closed over completely.

How could a guy look so good?

It wasn't as if she hadn't met handsome guys before. Guys in her father's social circle had money, had used it to pamper and preen. Not in a sissy manner but in the new wave of metrosexual manicures and facials for men keen to look their best. Leon had been striking in his own way but compared to Roman? The two were as different as the Palazzo and camping.

Hoping she wasn't drooling, she managed to put one foot in front of the other and make it all the way down the aisle, enjoying his chivalry when he stood.

'You made it.'

'Was there ever any doubt?'

He held up a hand, wavered it side to side a little. 'In my business it pays not to be overconfident.'

She laughed at that. 'If there's one thing you don't have it's a lack of confidence.'

'Maybe it only extends to certain areas of my life?' He held out his hand and she took it as he guided her down into the softest leather. 'Like wooing beautiful women?'

'Something I'm sure you've had loads of practice with.'

Pretending to ponder, he winked. 'Hey, extreme sports is my life. I never know when my last moment on this earth is so I make the most of the ones I have.'

She envied him that, his blasé, live-for-the-moment attitude to life. Totally foreign to a girl who'd spent her life evaluating choices, from what she wore in the morning to what she ate for fear of putting on weight in front of the ever-present intruding cameras.

Had she ever been spontaneous? Had she ever truly lived in the moment until last night?

Doubtful, and as Roman sank into the plush lounge next to her she was determined to live by his motto over the next few days and enjoy every moment they had together. No matter how fleeting, how transient, she'd go for it.

'Want to know something?'

He nodded, slung his arm across the back of the

lounge again, his fingertips grazing her bare shoulders and sending a river of promise flooding through her.

'I like your outlook. It's refreshing and inherently honest.'

She caught a fleeting glimpse of pain before he blinked and it was gone.

'It's also dangerous and reckless and can get me killed.'

His carefree expression closed off. Why the sudden turnaround? As if he was trying to talk down his passion?

She wanted to delve, wanted to probe for answers behind his sudden reticence. But that wouldn't be conducive to living in the moment and impulsiveness and passion, three things she really wanted to concentrate on, so she aimed for levity.

'Getting behind the wheel of a car is more likely to get you killed than anything else but you do that, right?'

He was back to his suave best, his fingers caressed her shoulder. 'Guess now isn't the best time to tell you I ride a motorcycle too?'

She smiled. 'I'd expect nothing less—fits the image totally.'

'Bet you see me as some risk-taking adventurer hooked on firsts?'

'Nothing wrong with firsts,' she said, remembering last night and blushing again.

Tuned in to her thoughts and giving her time to reassemble her scattered wits, he said, 'I'm guessing this isn't your first time on a private jet?'

She nodded, knowing he was only making polite conversation but wishing she didn't have to discuss her past. Apart from making a determined new start, how boring would her old life seem to an adventurer like him?

'You guessed right.'

'Did you travel much as a kid?'

'Yeah, a fair bit.'

He grinned at her brief responses. 'From your less than effusive answers you don't want to talk about your past?'

'Something like that.'

How could she explain without sounding like a spoiled brat disenchanted with her previous life, when her reasons for discontent were so much deeper than that?

He didn't know her beyond what they'd shared physically and as memorable as that was—and the promise of magic over the next few days—this wasn't the time for sharing deep, dark secrets.

'You don't have to talk about it if you don't want to but sometimes exorcising old demons is the best way to move forward.'

She stared at him in amazement. For all his flirty comments and sexy smiles, Roman had a depth to him that was seriously appealing.

'I don't want to bore you.'

Taking hold of her hand, he squeezed it encouragingly. 'You could never do that.'

Enjoying the feel of his strong, warm hand wrapped around hers, she said, 'Really? Bet you're just dying to hear about my life during Dad's eight-year term in office. How the last five years of my teens was spent under scrutiny from PR people, watching what I did, vetting what I said in interviews, choosing my wardrobe every morning.'

He grimaced and threaded his fingers through hers. 'Sounds like the pits.'

'It was.'

But that wasn't the worst of it and now she'd started down this rocky road, she had to tell him more.

Not all of it though, for the last thing she needed right now was to rehash the awfulness of having her divorce splashed across the media and everything from her morals to her family values publicly ridiculed.

'You know what annoys me the most? The fact that I went along with it all.'

'You had no choice.'

'Not at the beginning but, after a while, being the obedient, subservient perfect daughter became so ingrained I just coasted along, doing what was expected because it was easy.'

'Easy is good.'

She scanned his face to see if he was making a joke but the sombreness pinching his usually smiling mouth told her he understood.

'My finance career was a mistake. My marriage was a mistake.'

Releasing her hand, he brushed a strand of hair back off her face and tucked it behind her ear with a tenderness that brought a lump to her throat.

'Pretty hard to learn if we don't make mistakes.'

'True, but I feel like I've wasted the first twenty-seven years of my life being someone I'm not.'

She'd just voiced her biggest fear: that in sacrificing her needs, her wants, for the greater good of her family, she'd lost herself and maybe wouldn't be able to find herself now.

'Finding a new job in a field I love is a start but I sometimes wonder if the real me will ever emerge.'

The moment the words spilled from her mouth she knew she'd said too much, divulging too much too soon.

A guy in Australia for a short time, a guy to have a fling with, wasn't interested in her deep-seated fears.

He remained silent, his expression thoughtful, reinforcing she'd blurted out way too much to be cool.

Before she could come up with some flyaway comment to lighten the mood he scooted closer and slid an arm around her waist, holding her close while tipping up her chin with the other hand, leaving her no option but to look at him.

'The real you is the woman I was with last night. A vibrant, generous, spontaneous woman willing to explore her sensual side, a woman open to giving and receiving pleasure, a woman taking a risk on the unknown, grabbing opportunities with both hands.'

Her eyelids flickered shut as he brushed a soft kiss across her lips, his words filling her with pride.

'You're spectacular, Ava, and I'm honoured to be part of your self-discovery quest.'

In that moment it hit her, what he must think, and her eyes flew open as she jerked back.

'I'm not using you, if that's what you think.'

'It's okay if you are,' he murmured, the hint of truth behind his statement making her recoil.

She didn't use people. She was gracious and polite and thoughtful. She put the needs of others before her own.

Correction, she used to. Maybe Roman was right? Maybe it was okay to want something for herself? Not that she was using him exactly. She preferred to think of him as a delicious side benefit to exploring her new self.

Wrinkling her nose, she said, 'I'm not a user. But I'm not averse to using this…this thing between us to help my new self emerge.'

'I'm happy with that.'

And he kissed her to prove it, a long, hot, deep kiss with enough sizzle to make her forget every word they'd just exchanged, along with her name.

Ava who? was her last thought as he eased her back against the butter-soft leather and proceeded to give her another lesson in using the thing between them to further her cause.

CHAPTER SIX

Ava had always found air travel monotonous and dull.

Not any more.

The memory of what she'd done with Roman on the jet heated her cheeks more than the high humidity as she stepped onto the tarmac at Coolangatta Airport.

'Transport's taken care of,' he said, sliding a hand into hers as if it were the most natural thing in the world, while she darted a frantic glance towards the terminal before deliberately relaxing.

She'd left most of the gutter journalists who'd made her life hell for the past few weeks back in Canberra so she should be safe from prying eyes here. Time for a fresh start, free from looking over her shoulder every two seconds.

Glancing at her hand in Roman's, boy, had she got that fresh start and more.

It helped she'd cut her hair and had streaky blonde foils skilfully woven through it, plus gained a few pounds. The weight added softness to her previously angular frame and she loved not having to watch every single calorie cooked and blanched and trimmed of fat by a personal chef.

If Roman's reaction to her new curves was any indication, she wasn't the only one appreciating the extra kilos.

Misinterpreting her baulking, Roman glanced at her. 'Too hot for you?'

He was talking about the tropical Queensland weather but, buoyed by their recent escapade, she sent him a coy smile.

'I can handle it.'

He raised a brow at her innuendo and laughed. 'I'm liking this new you better and better.'

He tugged on her hand and she happily fell into step beside him, proud when covert glances slid their way. Paparazzi she loathed; envious women she could handle.

And there were plenty of them, normal, red-blooded women who couldn't help but stare at six feet plus of gorgeousness.

She wondered if Roman noticed the swathe he cut through the terminal but he seemed oblivious, his gaze searching for someone.

'There's our man,' he said, pointing to a suited chauffeur holding up a placard with GIANAKIS in bold print.

'You're Greek?'

The fact she didn't know his surname until now would've seriously distressed the old her. But the new, improved model liked the fact she'd hooked up with an incredibly sexy guy without the formalities of surnames.

He didn't know hers for that matter and she couldn't care less. If he was up on world politics he'd know it anyway, for Earl Beckett had been a fair, well-loved prime minister renowned for his patriotism and sense of humour. Pity that hadn't extended to home so much.

And the fact the Beckett name was so well known here was the reason she'd be using Ava Beck as a pseudonym. Everything she achieved in her new life would be courtesy of her achievements, not her name.

'Mum's Greek.'

'And your dad?'

'English apparently.'

A studied blankness settled over his face, a well-practised mask if the speed in which it descended was any indication as she silently cursed her blundering.

Shunning her past was one thing, but forgetting the etiquette drummed into her at finishing school? Unforgivable.

Hating the prolonged silence after the closeness they'd established on the jet, she rushed on. 'Sorry for prying—'

'Don't apologise. My questionable paternity is something I dealt with a long time ago.'

But as he strode towards the chauffeur and she all but ran to keep up she knew he was wrong. By the rigid shoulders, tensed jaw and grim-set mouth, Roman hadn't dealt with his paternity issues, not at all.

And while it was none of her business, and went against her new motto to live in the moment, she wondered what really went on behind that handsome face and wished he felt comfortable enough with her to blab the way she had on the flight.

Who knew, maybe he'd let her in over the next few days? Interviewing the guy was guaranteed to give her insight into more than his love of extreme sports.

Though the real question should be did she want to get close? And what would be the consequences for her naïve heart if she did?

Roman had stuffed up.

Sure, he'd had good intentions securing a trial for

Ava with Rex and he'd been looking forward to continuing what they'd started in her hotel room that night in Melbourne.

But having good motives and craving good sex were a far cry from how she'd made him feel on the jet: as if he wanted to blurt his whole damn life story and there was no way he'd go there.

The next few days were about work for Ava, checking out sporting hot spots for him and indulging the powerful chemistry between them.

Nothing more, nothing less.

The more time he spent with her, the more he wondered what kind of a jackass her ex was. It had been bugging him since last night when they'd had sex and now after their mind-blowing encounter on the jet: what sort of an idiot wouldn't appreciate a sensual, lively woman like Ava?

She'd mentioned he'd been a family friend and there'd been limited sparks but hell, the guy must've been a eunuch not to want to jump Ava every second.

He'd had *friends with benefits* over the years, longstanding casual friendships with women who turned him on. And while he wouldn't put Ava in that class with her ex, he couldn't comprehend how the guy hadn't ravaged his wife every chance he got.

Then she'd said all that stuff about not really knowing who she was and sacrificing her life for her dad and he'd wanted to strangle the men in her life for denting her confidence. Though considering what they'd done on the jet, he liked the fact she was heading down the road of self-discovery with him as a passenger.

If he hadn't stuffed up enough by allowing her to creep under his guard, he'd taken it a step further, letting her innocuous question about his father get to him.

She'd seen right through him, hadn't bought his brush off. And after the way she'd opened up to him on the plane, he'd felt like a real jerk. Not that he wanted to discuss his paternity, or lack of, with a virtual stranger, it was how he'd handled it that really peed him off.

'You're awfully quiet.'

Ava's soft, cultured voice stopped him from stepping further down the path of remembrance, a path he'd trodden all too often with Estelle kicking and screaming every step of the way.

'Mentally planning.'

'Planning what?'

With an exaggerated wink he knew would lighten the unexpected sombreness since his paternal gaff, he said, 'You'll see.'

She smiled as he'd intended and his chest considerably lightened at the sight of that delectable mouth curving upwards.

'Should I be worried?'

'Very.'

He jerked a thumb over his shoulder towards the tarmac. 'What happened on that jet? Call it a prelude.'

A delicate pink stained her cheeks, highlighting the incredible blueness of her eyes.

'To what?'

'A few days you'll never forget.'

He kissed her to prove it.

Ava slid into the back seat of the white limousine sedan and resisted the urge to lie across the pewter leather seats.

She needed a lie down, desperately. Roman had promised her a few days she'd never forget…she practically squirmed at the thought, remembering what he'd done to her at the hotel, and again on the jet...

'Comfortable?'

Knowing her cheeks would be lit like a beacon courtesy of her thoughts, she nodded.

'Rest up, you're going to need your strength.'

Risking a quick glance his way, she couldn't help but laugh.

'Stop looking at me like that.'

'Like this, you mean?'

He leered at her and wiggled his eyebrows until she laughed.

'You've got me all hot and bothered,' she murmured, hoping the chauffeur didn't have bionic hearing.

Leaning across the roomy back seat, he murmured in her ear. 'That's the idea.'

Needing some time to cool down before she melted all over these very expensive leather seats, she nudged him away with her elbow.

'I've got a very important article to write, don't forget.'

He folded his arms and tried a mock frown, which lost its impact with the corners of his mouth twitching.

'I've got work to do too, making sure you paint me in the best light possible.'

'Good, glad we're both clear.'

He beckoned her with his finger and she edged forwards warily.

'We're also clear that it pays to mix business with pleasure, right?'

He ran a fingertip down her bare forearm, the fine hairs snapping to attention like the rest of her body.

Sheesh, for a girl who'd never been all that interested in sex it was all she could think about now. And while she could blame it all on Roman, she should be thanking him instead. She'd never felt as alive as she had the last twenty-four hours. To think, it was only the beginning...

'Hold that thought,' he said, his knowing expression making her blush all over again.

And she did, tuning out the chauffeur's mini-documentary as he extolled the virtues of Miami High's Hollywood-esque sign on a hill, the wonders of millionaire row on Mermaid Beach, the attractions of Broadbeach and the cosmopolitan nightlife of Surfers Paradise.

Thankfully Roman kept up a steady conversation with the zealous driver, leaving her to mull and ponder and wonder how a staid, sedate divorcee had been thrust into a whirlwind fling with the hottest guy ever.

When she didn't come up with any answers, she thanked fate anyway.

The moment Rex had given her a trial run in a field she coveted, Ava had opened that part of her mind long suppressed and started to use her writing brain again.

Her imagination slowly stretched and flexed, closely observing the world around her, describing everything she saw from wizened old men to harried mums yanking recalcitrant toddlers along. Phrases flitted through her head constantly, word snapshots of a rich, vibrant environment.

She wanted to write. She had a chance and she'd make sure this article on Roman was the best darn thing she'd ever produced. Probably not very difficult considering the last time she'd written anything was for her Year Twelve Lit exam.

With her critical eye on high alert, words fizzed and

bubbled and coalesced in her mind the instant the doormen opened the monstrous glass doors and she set foot inside Palazzo Versace.

Breathtaking, superlative, indulgent and *opulent* sprang to mind and her fingers itched with the urge to start writing again.

She loved this buzz, this pre-writing state where sentences or paragraphs or opening lines shimmered into consciousness, as she wondered for the umpteenth time how she could've shoved all this aside to do the *right* thing.

'It's gorgeous,' she said, trying not to appear like a gawking tourist as she did a slow three-sixty.

'Sure is.'

Her wide-eyed gaze landed on Roman, who wasn't looking at the foyer.

'You don't have to try those lines any more, remember?'

She lightly touched his arm, her fingertips yearning to do so much more. 'I'm yours.'

Momentary alarm turned his eyes ebony as she quickly amended, 'For the next few days.'

She had her answer right there to the nebulous question floating around in the back of her head: what would happen beyond the next week if things between them deepened?

Roman hadn't spelled it out as such; he hadn't needed to, they'd both known the terms of this going in.

Brief fling. Limited to days. No regrets.

So why did that flare of alarm hurt?

Desperate to move onto safer ground, she swept her arm wide. 'I like the neo-classical look.'

His eyes narrowed imperceptibly, shrewdly assessing, as he saw straight through her lame attempt at changing the subject.

'I like the sofas.' He paused, sending her a loaded glance that curled her toes. 'A couple could get mighty comfortable on those.'

Shaking her head at his exaggerated wink, she focused on the sofas in question, admiring their beauty more than the comfort factor.

Gold embossed and circular, they featured beautiful magenta orchids in the middle as a striking offset. Truly spectacular, along with the signature cushions in shades of mint green, pale blue and tangerine, the gold and cream marble floors, the elaborate mosaics, the giant crystal chandelier overhead, the ebony grand piano and the huge circular table dead centre of the entrance doors bearing a detailed floral arrangement that drew the eye.

'You're taking mental notes?'

She nodded. 'It's the writer in me.' She tapped her temple. 'Now I'm switched on up here, can't turn off.'

'One of the many things I admire about you, your creativity,' he said, lifting her spirits by knowing the exact right thing to say at the right time.

Flustered by how he made her feel, she blurted her first thought.

'I haven't even written my first article. How would you know?'

His killer smile forewarned an incoming repartee missile she had no hope of avoiding.

'There are many ways to demonstrate creativity.'

An instant image of how they'd ensured privacy on the jet, by sliding together compartments similar to those in first class on commercial airliners, and the

subtle readjusting of clothes without disrobing to pleasure each other, reinforced his statement.

'As for your article, maybe I can get a sneak peek at
your literary talents while you're interviewing me?'

Lowering his voice, he added, 'You know, while
we're mixing business and pleasure.'

The word *pleasure* slid off his tongue like warm
honey and she shivered in anticipation. No way would
she get any work done with him looking over her shoulder and an errant thought suddenly struck.

'We've got separate rooms, right?'

His lips curved at her wary tone. 'Redundant, considering our arrangement—'

'I need my own space to work.'

Hating how panicked she sounded, a fact he found
infinitely amusing by his belligerent expression, she
toned it down a notch.

'And don't call it an arrangement. We're having a
fling. Much more exciting.'

She almost tossed her hair for good measure.

His grin made her want to throttle him but the
thought of placing her hands around his throat led to
more pleasurable thoughts of what she could do with
her hands on his body.

With a mocking half-salute, he said, 'Fling. Got it.'

'Shh, keep your voice down,' she hissed, old habits
dying hard as she quickly scanned the foyer for signs
of disguised reporters bearing recording devices.

His smile faded as she deliberately relaxed her tense
shoulders.

'You're not still harassed by paparazzi?'

'Lord, I hope not.'

Her fervent response garnered a long look and she
sighed. 'I've put up with being scrutinised and photo-

graphed and questioned for years. After a while the avoidance behaviour becomes ingrained.'

As for the rest…she suppressed a shudder at the memory of the full-page spreads devoted to her divorce.

'Know what you mean.'

He froze and, confused, she frowned. 'How?'

For a second she saw that flare of panic again, as if he'd said too much, before he blinked and erased it.

'Extreme sports gets its fair share of publicity. News hounds follow the elite around in any sport so I've seen it firsthand.'

A perfectly rational, logical explanation. Then why the conviction there was more behind his sound response?

'Is this going to be a problem for you? Us being seen together? Because if it is…'

Rather than being impressed by his concern, she hated that he'd given her an out. It meant this thing between them didn't mean much to him, that he could take or leave their time together and that stung as much as the blasé way he'd thrown it out there.

'It's not a problem,' she muttered, aiming for cool but sounding like a petulant kid regardless.

'Hey, you okay?'

She'd learned to hide her feelings many years ago, to mask her true emotions, to always, *always*, present a poised, confident mask to the world.

Someone could be watching was her dad's favourite indoctrinating phrase and she'd taken it to heart, initially practising for hours in front of a mirror to get her 'all's right with the world' face under control.

So where the heck was her famed emotional control now, when a lump the size of the chandelier overhead welled in her throat, making her want to blubber?

His hands sliding around her waist, gripping her firmly, didn't help.

'I want this, Ava, I do, but not at the expense of your career.'

He paused, as if searching for the right words, the first time she'd seen him as anything other than commanding, and the hint of uncertainty was what captured her attention the most.

'You're on trial, this is your first writing gig and I'll be damned if I screw that up for you, no matter how much I want you.'

His sincerity rattled her as much as his concern. For all his witty one-liners and constant flirting, Roman actually cared enough to put *her* career, *her* needs, ahead of his.

It blew her away.

No one had ever done that: not her dad, her mum, her ex-husband. Yet here was a guy she'd known for a day putting her first and it made her feel special for the first time ever.

Clearing her throat and hoping what she had to say wouldn't come out a squeak, she eyeballed him.

'I'm onto you.'

'You are?'

'Uh-huh. For all your roguish charm, you're actually a big softie.'

She didn't understand his fleeting relief as he nodded.

'Yeah, you're onto me.'

Releasing her arms, he patted his chest over his heart.

'Pure marshmallow in here.'

'Lucky I've got a sweet tooth.'

'Yeah, lucky.'

His kiss stole her breath but as she gave herself over to the pleasure of it she couldn't help but wonder if he'd used it as a distraction.

CHAPTER SEVEN

ROMAN paced his deluxe suite, desperate to shake off the uncharacteristic nerves.

Him? The guy who'd jumped off more buildings, more cliffs, more bridges than any other competitor in his field, the guy who held the skydiving, free-diving and scuba-diving records, the guy who'd mastered hang-gliding and snowboarding and street luge by his early teens?

He didn't do nerves. Ever. So why this uncertain, edgy feeling that just wouldn't quit?

He knew the reason behind it; he just didn't want to acknowledge it.

Ava.

Why the hell was he blurting little truths to her when he'd shut away those parts of him long ago? How was she getting under his skin so easily, a skin he'd deliberately thickened years ago?

He couldn't figure it out. What was it about the sweet, reserved girl that had him wanting to blurt out private thoughts best left unsaid? Had to be his lack of social life lately. For a guy who dated widely and extensively he'd been so wrapped up in his mum's problems he hadn't had time.

Not good.

He loved women. Loved the thrill of the chase, the appreciation they showed him, the attention, and while his dalliances never went past a few dates he enjoyed the closeness being with a woman brought.

Until now.

Being with Ava somehow moved beyond closeness, her unerring ability to home in on his innermost thoughts bordering on an intimacy he'd shied away from his entire life.

The smart thing to do would be to leave her a list of answers to common questions he'd been asked by the press in the past, then do a runner. Easy. He could have the jet refuelled and a limo ready with a few phone calls.

But the memory of Ava's blue eyes, glittering with excitement, dazed with passion, sparkling with anticipation, was difficult to ignore let alone forget and he cursed, flinging himself into a chair. He couldn't leave, not when her fledgling writing career hinged on her interviewing him.

He'd been where she was, a newbie in the field, used to feeling unloved and unwanted and not good enough, needing the vindication of his career to feel something other than crappy and he'd be damned if she continued to wallow.

He'd lost himself in the adrenalin rush of extreme sports to forget, to gain the recognition he craved and deserved.

But how would Ava get it when she was using a pseudonym and still looking over her shoulder for lurking paparazzi?

No, he couldn't leave. And once she'd written the article…if indulging Ava in the fling she wanted brought her half the rush free-falling from ten thousand feet brought him, she'd be on her way to shrugging off her past and embracing her future.

Ava sighed with pleasure as she sank into a comfy sofa in her deluxe suite. She'd stayed in hotels the world over from a young age but none had quite the impact of this one.

It was more than the impressive foyer or her lovely suite, decorated in rich royal blues and plump cushions and the signature ornate Versace filigree edging everything from the ceiling to teaspoons.

It was the overall ambiance, a general feeling of understated elegance, of subtle class, that enveloped her the moment she stepped through the doors and only intensified as she wandered through the hotel.

Of course, having Roman alongside to share the experience didn't hurt; though she'd been grateful to step into the privacy of her own room and out of his commanding, overwhelming presence. For that was how he made her feel at times: overwhelmed.

Everything seemed brighter and sharper and larger than life when she was with him and for a girl used to living in the shadows by choice lately it was almost too much. He was so…so…*vibrant*.

The creative part of her brain imagined him as the sun, with everyone in his sphere revolving around him. Corny, maybe, but he was that kind of guy. The last type of guy she could ever see herself with, which was why he was perfect for her now.

A fun, no-holds-barred fling was exactly what she wanted.

If there was one thing she'd learned over the last few weeks since the divorce it was to value her independence and no way would she give that up again in a hurry.

She had no aspirations to enter into another relationship, so a transient, hot, half-Greek adventurer entering her life for a brief moment in time seemed fortuitous.

Imagine her, Ava Beckett, daughter of the great Earl Beckett, having a fling?

Eighteen months ago she would've filed the thought away alongside her other pie-in-the-sky dreams like writing for a career. Thankfully, Leon had broached the subject they'd been avoiding since early in their two-year marriage: it wasn't working and did she want out?

She could remember the day so clearly: they'd been to a civilised afternoon tea at Government House, celebrating bravery honours for worthy recipients. She'd worn an understated, bland, below-the-knee ivory sheath dress; he'd worn his favourite suit.

They'd smiled and shook hands and said all the right things to all the right people but as the afternoon wore on so did her brittle façade.

How many of these functions had she attended, first as the prime minister's daughter and later as a politician's wife?

How many canapés and chardonnays had she consumed?

How many fake pleasantries and shallow conversations shared?

Too many to count and that afternoon something deep inside had cracked. Not that she'd said anything but Leon, usually more tuned in to his constituency than her, picked up on it and when they'd returned to their apartment he'd confronted her.

There'd been no harsh words, no accusations, just a clear-cut stating of facts. They'd fallen into an easy relationship in their late teens and fallen just as easily into a comfortable, expected marriage as young twenty-somethings.

There were no recriminations, no what-ifs, and for that she'd been grateful.

She'd been liberated while Leon had been exiled to a foreign post in Belgium. Not totally unexpected, considering the major fit her dad had when he learned of their plans to separate. But all her dad's bluster and temper had been no match for Leon's calm rationale and when Mum had nodded knowingly and laid a hand on Dad's shoulder, Ava had known everything would be okay.

Besides, a small part of her wondered if her dad's horror had been more about how his daughter's failed marriage would reflect on him than about any real caring for her feelings.

Though he'd been out of office a while, once a politician always a politician and her dad valued appearances above all else. It was why she'd gone into hiding once the story of her divorce had first broken, when the media vultures had descended, hounding her every second of every day, thrusting microphones into her face, hurling questions and later accusations.

Was Leon having an affair?

Was she seeing anyone else?

Could she not have children, was that the problem?

Horrible, intrusive questions that intensified the longer she remained silent and that was when they really notched up the heat, smearing her reputation with their invented lies.

She didn't blame Leon for heading to Belgium, the farther the better from the merciless, repetitive questioning. But she did blame her dad every time he got asked a question and he eyeballed a camera, muttering his usual stoic 'no comment'.

Why hadn't he defended her? Stood up for her?

He'd done it for the party faithful, fellow politicians who'd indulged in real-life scandals, yet couldn't say one word in his daughter's defence?

It hurt almost as much as the rubbish the press had printed about her, if not more. Crazy thing was using a pseudonym now wasn't just a show of independence without the pull of the Beckett name but out of a respect for the man who was still her dad, no matter how much his career had ruled her life growing up.

Pressing the pads of her fingers against her eyelids, she blinked several times, opened her eyes, her gaze landing on the carved Versace face above a king-size bed in the bedroom opposite.

Its expression benign, it seemed to be smiling at her, encouraging her to follow her dreams and with an uncharacteristic whoop she leapt to her feet and danced around the room, truly excited by her prospects for the future.

Freedom. Anonymity. There was nothing like it and she intended on making the most of every second with her new man for however long it lasted.

As for her new job, once she stopped bopping around, she'd better flip open her laptop and start flexing her fingers. Making a list of strict, factual questions was the only way she'd keep Roman on track.

Or was she the one with a deep-seated fear of being derailed?

Patting her belly, Ava groaned. 'That was categorically the best seafood buffet I've ever had.'

And the best dinner companion she'd ever had as she

gazed across the table, the candlelight casting alluring shadows across Roman's handsome face, making her fingers itch to reach out and stroke his cheek.

'Agreed,' he said, forking the last piece of chocolate cake into his mouth. 'Though how I'm going to fit into my wetsuit after this is beyond me.'

Wetsuit...moulding to his body...

Her heart gave an odd little pitter-patter as she remembered exactly how his body looked without anything at all.

Raising her wine glass, she leaned forward. 'If you need a hand?'

He laughed at her outrageously lame attempt at flirting.

'Only if you promise to come wake-boarding with me.'

'Not a chance.'

He tsked-tsked. 'You're a sporting neophyte.'

Feigning outrage, she waggled a finger. 'I'll have you know I've taken great interest in Aussie Rules since I've moved to Melbourne. And I watch the tennis. And the occasional golf.'

He snorted. 'That's because you like perving on broad-shouldered men in tight shorts.'

Laughter twitched her lips. 'Okay, so you're onto me. Maybe I'll come watch you get pulled behind a boat on a ridiculously small board? Let me know whether to pack my binoculars or not.'

He shook his head. 'Neophyte and a perv.'

She loved this, the smiles and laughter and light-hearted quips. Dinner with Leon had consisted of routine questions—how was your day? What are your plans for tomorrow?—and expected answers: 'fine' and 'work, the usual'. There'd been no banter or jokes or flirting, just two people co-existing in the same house.

Considering how warm and fuzzy being with Roman made her feel, she should've got out a long time ago.

Snapping her fingers, she said, 'This *neophyte* is going to paint you in a very favourable light in her article if you're lucky, so be nice.'

He saluted. 'Got it. Don't want to get the journo off-side.'

Disgust twisted her gut at being lumped in with the bloodhounds that'd made her life a misery over the last month but she hid her discomfort behind a small smile.

No way would she ever be like them: inventing drivel when they couldn't get the truth, printing rubbish disguised as *fact*. Uh-uh, when she wrote her freelance articles she'd stick to verifiable data all the way.

She liked that *Globetrotter* was a respected magazine, read worldwide for its travel articles and interesting interviews. The fact she'd been given the job of writing one of those interviews blew her away. And if she nailed it…writing on a regular basis, writing for a job, would be incredibly, stupefyingly brilliant.

'This journo has a huge list of questions to ask you, the first being why you need publicity anyway.'

A shadow passed over his face before his characteristic charming smile was back, making her wonder if she'd imagined it.

'You said you'd seen some extreme sport games on television?'

'You mean that Olympic-style event for crazy people who want to break their necks jumping off buildings and bridges?'

His eyes narrowed but he couldn't dim the amused glint.

'You're mocking me.'

She held up her thumb and index finger an inch apart. 'Maybe just a little?'

'Anyway...' he made a zipping motion over his lips; yeah, as if that would shut her up when she was enjoying sparring with him '...marketing companies get behind it, competitors love it, fans flock in droves.'

'So the article?'

'My employer wants to run something along similar lines in Europe so the more I get my head on the TV, radio and print media, the better.'

Another shudder rippled through her. What he'd just described was her biggest nightmare.

'You're the face of your sports' governing body?'

The shadow reappeared, darker this time, looming over him like a storm cloud, creasing his brow, clenching his hands, which he quickly hid beneath the table.

'Yeah, so I need all the good publicity I can get, which is where you come in.'

The investigative writing side of her brain had a hard time damping down her curiosity. He loved his sports, loved his job from all accounts when they'd first met so why the reluctance to discuss the publicity angle? Had Roman been burned by the paparazzi too?

From what she'd learned last night, doubtful. She'd looked him up on the Internet to get a feel for what questions to ask him and the amount of hits on his name was staggering. The guy was a serious media hound, attracting coverage the world over. Considering his looks and physique, not terribly surprising, but from the scope of articles in everything from sporting journals to gossip mags it looked as if he seriously encouraged publicity. Why the recalcitrance now?

'I hear you.' Eager for the twinkle in his eyes to return, she pretended to ponder. 'What you're saying is you want me to highlight you against a backdrop of extreme sports, highlighting how variables aren't always constant, like rock quality for climbers, snow conditions for snowboarders, wave height and shape for surfers, that kind of thing.'

She laughed at his comedic incredulity.

'You lied about being a neophyte.'

'Yep.'

His speculative gaze swept over her, his lips curving as if he liked what he saw.

'With this much cheek, who knows what you'll write about me?'

'Just the facts.'

'I like the sound of that.'

His shoulders relaxed and the crease between his brows faded, his relief obvious and confirming her earlier suspicions. Had some journo done a number on him too? She'd found nothing terribly damning during her online search last night but maybe he'd had it pulled? A guy in his position, as CEO of a sporting governing body, couldn't afford bad press. But would he have that much influence to have a nasty article removed from cyberspace?

She'd heard that once something hit the cyber-world it was there for ever and though she'd deliberately not searched herself on the Internet she knew what she'd find if she did: not the numerous charity benefits she'd attended or the money she'd raised, not the kids' halfway house she was a patron of and regular visitor. Oh no, she'd find those disgusting, slanderous articles on her divorce front and centre.

They'd painted Leon out to be the slighted husband, cuckolded by a cold, frigid ice maiden.

'No wonder he left, she's the ice princess' was one of the nicer things they'd printed. She knew why too.

She'd resented being under the spotlight her entire life; resented the press intrusion every time she stepped out of the front door with her family, resented the constant keeping up of appearances, resented her lack of a normal teenage life.

She'd resented it all and she'd never been comfortable in the media spotlight, had gone out of her way to stand back and let her dad, and later Leon, deal with the press.

While they'd been jovial and effusive, she'd been reserved and aloof, happy for them to do all the talking. She'd shunned countless interview offers from newspapers and magazines, valuing what little privacy she had.

Somehow, when her marriage had hit the wall, those same news hounds had decided it was payback time, persecuting her for her years of silence with invented garbage that still stung despite her efforts to forget it.

'What you thinking about?'

Annoyed she'd allowed herself to be distracted, she shook her head. 'Mentally running through the list of questions I've got lined up for you.'

He reached across the table and smoothed a finger between her brows. 'By that frown, should I be scared?'

Laughing off his concern, she swiped at his hand. 'Terrified.'

'How about I save you some time?'

He held up a hand and ticked off points. 'Favourite food is moussaka, favourite song Lenny Kravitz's "Fly Away", favourite sport is B.A.S.E. jumping.'

Unexpected apprehension quivered through her at

the thought of this amazing guy jumping off anything with only a parachute to break his fall.

'Don't you have to do at least one jump from a building, antenna, bridge and cliff to qualify as a B.A.S.E. jumper?' She swallowed her nausea at jumping off anything other than the edge of a pool.

'Yeah, cool, huh?'

His smile warmed her better than the sticky date pudding and hot caramel sauce she'd had for dessert.

'I can think of other words to describe it.'

'Hey, don't knock it 'til you've tried it.'

She held up her hands and shook her head. 'No way. I can't even look at a roller coaster without feeling sick.'

His eyebrows shot up. 'You don't like fast rides?'

'Got it in one.'

He beckoned her closer and she leaned forward, savouring the subtle scent of sunshine clinging to his skin.

'Maybe you've just had the wrong guy at the helm all those other rides?'

Smiling at his cockiness, she laid a hand on his chest and gently shoved him back.

'I don't care who's at the helm, I'm not getting on any death traps to begin with. And I'm certainly not leaping off anything higher than a footstool.'

'Bet you'll change your mind.'

'Bet I won't.'

He tapped the side of his nose and winked. 'Never bet against an adrenalin junkie. Everything's a challenge to surmount.'

'Well, good luck with this one because the closest you'll get me near the top of a cliff is watching it on the telly.'

'We'll see.'

By his smug expression, he was in little doubt she'd

fall in with whatever nefarious plan his ruminations landed on.

Sure, the guy was sexy and sweet and totally sizzling, but if he thought she'd indulge in any of his extreme jumping/speeding/whatever, she had two words for him.

Like hell.

'Like hell I'm jumping out of this thing.'

Ava's fingers convulsed around the steel bench and her butt scooted backwards until she encountered solid plane wall; a wall that vibrated and hummed, indicating exactly how high they were in the air.

She should've known not to trust Roman, especially when he'd virtually jumped at the challenge over dinner last night.

He'd pretended to be sweet and lovely and understanding when he'd walked her back to her room and agreed to her one night of solid prep work before they indulged their passion for the other nights; when in fact he was probably dying to get back to his room to plan this.

'You can't not do your first parachute jump now you've come this far.'

Her jaw dropped as she risked a glance out of the window, the thought of hurtling through the air at speeds defying man, with nothing more than a piece of silk tied to a few strings to break her fall, exacerbating her bone-deep fear.

'I agreed to a scenic flight over the Gold Coast.'

She jabbed a shaky finger at the cloudless blue sky.

'I did NOT agree to jump off a plane into that!'

He shrugged. 'Shame. I thought an adventurous girl like you would be up for anything.'

And just like that he pushed her buttons. Deliberately, of course, and they both knew it, but what he'd said rang true.

This was the new her: adventurous, taking risks. And while a parachute jump terrified her, she knew she'd regret not doing it more; for if she didn't tandem jump with this guy she'd never do it in the future.

Grabbing his hand, she squeezed until her knuckles turned white.

'Tell me you won't let go of my hand the whole time.'

'Promise.'

He squeezed it for good measure. It did little to quell her rollicking belly or thundering heart.

Thankfully, he didn't speak as they geared up, giving her time to assemble a rapidly decreasing supply of courage.

Think of the article.

Think of the depth this experience will add if you can write about a firsthand extreme sport experience with the guy you're interviewing.

Think of being on trial in a dream job.

Sadly, while she did think all those things she also thought about how the heck she'd keep her breakfast in her stomach when they jumped.

Her body co-operated with his instructions, stepping into the suit, getting harnessed up, standing still like a rigid robot as he triple-checked everything, talking her through every step of the jump in a low, soothing voice.

How a harness would attach her to him, how he wore a drogue parachute, which deployed shortly after they jumped to decrease terminal velocity, and how he'd activate the main parachute.

She heard the words but her brain refused to assimilate. She'd somehow switched onto autopilot, doing everything he asked while a silent scream wedged in her throat, a loud, resounding 'no-o-o!'

'We're up.'

She recoiled as they edged towards the door, wishing she could miraculously be vetoed by the pilot for being too inexperienced, too shaky, too terrified.

'You're not going to back out now? You've come so far,' he murmured in her ear, saying the right thing again as she sucked in a breath, another, before forcing one foot in front of the other.

If Roman didn't have her hand in a death grip she would've backed out but he gave her no option as she stood in front of him, determinedly avoiding looking at the sky beyond the door.

She'd once heard about the G forces involved when going really, really fast and while she didn't understand what a G force was she knew it couldn't be good.

'I'll be with you every step of the way,' he said as they reached the door and she braced, unaware of the metal harness joining them or the fact an expert had her back, unaware of everything but how unnatural it was to jump out of a plane.

She couldn't breathe as they hovered in the door, the wind rushing her face adding to the surrealism as every cell in her body screamed to escape while she still could.

But the time for escape was long past as Roman began a countdown: *10...9...8...*

Okay, she could do this, but as she was slowly acclimatising to the upcoming terror Roman urged her forward and they fell out.

She screamed as the force of the wind pressed her

back against him, a scream suffocated as her stomach climbed vertically into her throat.

They plunged, free-falling for horrific seconds.

Death had to be imminent.

Yet as she gritted her teeth, squeezed her eyes shut and prayed, her body yanked upwards as a chute unfurled and a funny thing happened.

She realised what she was doing.

In the midst of her abject fear and roiling tummy and trembling limbs, a huge surge of pride swelled alongside the adrenalin and she reluctantly prised her eyes open.

And promptly bit back another scream.

A patchwork quilt of indigo ocean and emerald fields and roads criss-crossing like toy tracks lay out before her and if she weren't so petrified she'd plunge to her death any second, this might've been kind of fun.

She never would've had the guts to do something like this, had been so stuck in her sedate ways it wouldn't have entered her head to take a scenic flight let alone do a tandem jump.

Yet here she was and while she wouldn't do it again in a hurry she decided to enjoy the terrifying buzz while it lasted.

As a larger parachute unfolded above them and they drifted towards earth she deliberately kept her eyes open, desperately swallowing to send her heart back to where it belonged.

Despite the tolerable speed at which they were travelling the ground seemed to be rising up to meet them at a hair-raising pace and she screamed again as they came into land in an open field, her legs managing not to buckle as they touched down, both of them running until Roman tapped her on the shoulder to slow down.

It wasn't until that moment she realised he hadn't let go of her other hand the entire time, just as she'd asked, but it wasn't 'til they'd stopped that she could breathe again.

She waited until he unbuckled her before turning, ready to flay him. But the moment she locked gazes with him, her verbal spray died. His eyes gleamed with admiration and approval and something suspiciously like genuine caring.

'I'm so proud of you.'

He leaned in and kissed her, a gentle kiss that didn't undermine her half as much as his appreciation of how much this had meant to her.

Tears stung her eyes and she blinked rapidly, not wanting to cry and ruin the moment. She hadn't cried after her divorce, she'd be damned if she cried now.

'Hey, I'm the one who should be tearing up, what with the way you've broken every bone in my hand.'

He wriggled his fingers to emphasise her death grip and she smiled through her tears, just as he'd intended.

'You'll live.'

Releasing his hand, she tentatively patted it. 'Besides, even if I had cracked a bone or two, it'd be entirely your fault.'

'A promise is a promise.' His eyes clouded before clearing. 'I promised to hold your hand the whole time and I came good.'

'Actually, I may need that hand again to help me get back to the terminal.'

She took a step forward to prove her point, her knees wobbling so badly she would've fallen if he hadn't reached out to her.

'Look up.'

Squinting against all that endless blue, she shook her head.

'Trust me, I don't need a reminder of my madness…' She trailed off, gobsmacked, as the enormity of what she'd just done sank in.

She'd actually jumped out of a plane.

All because of this man.

Lowering her gaze, she touched his cheek. 'Thank you.'

'You're welcome.'

Smart guy. He didn't ask why or what for; his understanding smile said it all.

'Ready for some hang-gliding or barefoot waterskiing next?'

Wincing, she shook her head. 'I think tai chi's more my speed after that.'

He nudged her. 'Come on, live a little.'

Holding his stare, she said, 'I intend to. Back at the hotel. Later.'

She wasn't surprised when they rushed through the post-jump procedures. A tandem parachute jump might have produced some serious adrenalin but they both knew the biggest thrill couldn't come soon enough.

FREE Merchandise is 'in the Cards' for you!

Dear Reader,

We're giving away FREE MERCHANDISE!

Seriously, we'd like to reward you for reading this novel by giving you **FREE MERCHANDISE** worth over \$20. And no purchase is necessary!

You see the Jack of Hearts sticker above? Paste that sticker in the box on the Free Merchandise Voucher inside. Return the Voucher promptly...and we'll send you valuable Free Merchandise!

Thanks again for reading one of our novels—and enjoy your Free Merchandise with our compliments!

Pam Powers

Pam Powers

P.S. Look inside to see what Free Merchandise is **"in the cards"** for you!

H-P-02/12

BUSINESS REPLY MAIL
FIRST-CLASS MAIL   PERMIT NO. 717   BUFFALO, NY

POSTAGE WILL BE PAID BY ADDRESSEE

THE READER SERVICE
PO BOX 1867
BUFFALO NY 14240-9952

NO POSTAGE
NECESSARY
IF MAILED
IN THE
UNITED STATES

▲ If offer card is missing write to: The Reader Service, P.O. Box 1867, Buffalo, NY 14240-1867 or visit www.ReaderService.com ▲

CHAPTER EIGHT

ROMAN knew the after-effects of an adrenalin rush well. The buzz, the high, the invincibility, the feeling you could take on the world.

He was addicted to the guaranteed feel-good buzz that ensured he stayed on top, stayed the best, stayed focused on conquering the next big thing.

Medical experts had argued with him that the rush wasn't due to adrenalin being released as a response to fear but more to do with the increased levels of dopamine, serotonin and endorphins following high exertion.

Whatever the cause, he didn't care, he'd take it. Time and time again.

So why did he experience the same rush earlier today watching Ava battle her fears and do a tandem jump?

There'd been minimal exertion on his part, he'd merely supported her through it, yet when the jump had finished and she'd looked at him in wide-eyed wonder he'd felt the same heart-pounding exhilaration he did following a B.A.S.E. jump or skydive or mountain boarding. What was with that?

He'd been so proud of her he'd wanted to crush her to him and never let go.

Right about then was when *his* fear kicked in, for he didn't do for ever.

Depending on the sports he loved for gratification, you bet. Depending on people? No way. He'd be better off jumping without a chute. Either way, he'd crash-land.

He'd needed to re-establish their relationship boundaries so he'd rung the hotel and set his plan in motion for when they returned. The sooner they remembered why they were together, the easier he'd rest.

Fling was good. Anything else? Not on the agenda.

'Thanks for today.'

Ava laid a hand on his arm as he was about to swipe the key card for his room and he stopped, hoping she'd like the next surprise he'd planned for her as much as today.

'You're welcome.'

He swiped the card, waited for the green light to blink and turned the door handle. 'Though I think you'll enjoy the rest of this more.'

'This?'

He loved how a simple arched eyebrow transformed her to imperious princess in a second.

'This.'

He flung open the door, suitably chuffed by her gasp.

'Wow.'

She stepped into the room and he followed, impressed with what the hotel had managed on short notice.

Tealight candles in glass holders were strategically placed throughout the room, their shadows dancing across the walls as he guided her into the suite.

'There's more.'

They stopped in the arch leading to the bedroom, where the king-size bed had been sprinkled with rose petals and more tealights created a sexy ambiance.

'How did you...?' She shook her head, her lips curving as she caught sight of the bath-tub, a huge spa bath built for two filled with what smelt suspiciously like honey.

Champagne propped in an ice bucket beside the bath, along with two crystal glasses, and the soft crooning of some soul singer filtered in the background.

He'd wanted to reward her; the hotel had come through for him.

'I didn't know what you liked so I went for a combined Romance and Honey Bliss Package.'

'I'm speechless,' she said, her eyes sweeping back to the tub and the tray of almond Florentines and melted chocolate sitting near the champagne.

'You deserve this.'

He came up behind her, slid his arms around her waist, revelling in her softness as she leaned back into him.

Tilting her head up, she smiled and the buzz was back, just as potent, just as scary.

'If this is what I get after jumping out of a plane, I've heard there's this really radical ride called the Claw, which spins three hundred and sixty degrees, nine storeys high, reaching zero gravity—'

He silenced her with a kiss, a passionate, no-holds-barred clash of lips and tongue that left them panting and moaning and frantic to get naked.

The setting deserved a slow stripping, a seductive peeling of top and shorts and panties to build anticipation and enhance sensation.

But the moment her hand zeroed in on his hard-on he lost it.

It had taken a lot to walk away from her last night and, still on an adrenalin high after the day they'd had, he needed to be inside her. Now.

Cotton ripped and satin shredded as their frantic hands made quick work of the barriers standing between them and bare skin.

Sheathing himself in record time, he hoisted her onto the black marble basin and drove into her, his adrenalin spiking again as she ground her pelvis against him, pleasuring herself.

Gritting his teeth, he stilled, watching her writhe and buck against him until she came, his name spilling from her lips in soft, murmured moans.

Unable to hold back any longer, he resumed his relentless quest for pleasure, driving into her until she scoured his back, their reflections in the mirror behind her heightening the eroticism.

Wrapping her legs around his waist, she clasped him so tightly he roared, his orgasm so intense he could've sworn he almost blacked out.

After several long seconds where he savoured the feel of being sheathed inside her, he finally eased back, to find a smug, satisfied grin on her flushed face.

Tracing his lips with a fingertip, she jerked her head towards the bath. 'Think I've worked up an appetite. Those Florentines are looking mighty good.'

'What about the chocolate dip?'

Her fingertip trailed down his jaw, along his neck and across his chest, where her nail scraped his nipple.

'I'm thinking we can save that for later...'

That buzz he had going on? Looked as if it'd last all night.

Ava could've coped with the honey and propolis and royal jelly infused bath.

She could've coped with the imported champagne and handmade Florentines and warmed chocolate dip.

She could've coped with Roman rubbing her languid limbs in honey-lemon body butter before taking his time exploring every curve, his skill as a lover taking her to ecstatic heights she'd never dreamed possible.

But what she couldn't cope with was waking in his arms, sated, satisfied and more secure than she'd ever felt.

Not good.

Being with Roman wasn't about security. It was about adventure and fun and short-term thrill. Last night had produced all that and more, and she put down her insatiability to the adrenalin coursing through her system.

They'd been wild last night, burning off all that energy, but now, cradled in his arms, feeling so protected?

Uh-uh, getting attached was the last thing she wanted or needed.

Yet for these brief few moments while he slumbered, she allowed herself to savour the illicit delight of being cradled in a pair of strong, muscular arms.

She'd never been a hugger, hadn't had much physical displays of affection as a kid. Her dad had favoured pats on the back and her mum cool pecks on the cheek, while Leon's lacklustre kisses had been filled with obligation rather than any grand passion.

Which made her wonder: was Roman such a talented charmer and exceptional lover that he created these sparks with everyone? Or was she in deeper than she professed?

She wouldn't tolerate that kind of fanciful thinking, wouldn't let anything or anyone stand in her way of gaining full independence. But for a second it was nice to think what she had with Roman was special.

Inching back a fraction, she studied him: the laugh lines at the corners of his eyes, the long lashes casting shadows on his cheeks, the sensual lips, the strong Mediterranean nose. His face had so much character, was so animated when he was awake that a person couldn't help but be drawn to him.

'Are you done staring yet?'

His eyelids snapped open and, unable to resist touching him, she cupped his cheek, relishing the rasp of stubble against her palm.

'It's okay to stare if you're thinking good thoughts.'

'In that case...' He whipped the top sheet off them and she squealed. 'There. That's better.'

His gaze roved over her, a slow, thorough perusal that left her breathless and not in the least bit self-conscious about her nakedness. Considering what they'd done last night, it was way too late for bashfulness.

'Yep. Definitely good thoughts,' he said, a second before his mouth fastened on her breast.

It was better this way, this purely physical expression of the tension between them, but as his lips trailed across her belly and lower, igniting her latent lust, she couldn't help but wonder what would happen if they had more than a few days together.

'You're seriously telling me this qualifies as research?'

Ava tied the sash of her robe tighter and mustered her best haughty glare as she stepped out of the elevator and Roman fell into step behind her.

'Of course. How else are you going to interview me if I'm not relaxed and right now the Salus Per Aquum is the best place for us to work.'

'You're mad,' she muttered, laughing as he tickled her ribs.

'You need me to answer questions, I need you to indulge me for an hour then I'm all yours.'

'Indulge you?'

'I've seen how you've been walking since the jump, thought it might be a good idea to get some of those muscles loosened up.'

His thoughtfulness impressed her as much as his powers of observation. She'd woken incredibly stiff today. Must've been all that excessive tension involved in clenching her muscles to keep her body from falling apart as she plummeted towards the ground.

'You're very tense,' he said, his hand straying from the small of her back lower, lingering over her butt.

'You're not helping,' she muttered, her admonition undermined by the little purr in the back of her throat as he caressed the curve of her butt.

'I intend to, later.' He bent to murmur in her ear, 'By answering each and every one of your questions. Forgiven?'

She removed his hand from her butt with regret. 'Not really. You need to stop arranging things for me. First the jump, now this.'

'Don't forget the bath package last night.'

He had her there. How could she admonish him for something so wonderful?

'You're lucky I don't extend the massage into a full-day retreat.'

He shook his head. 'You couldn't stay away from me that long.'

'Is that a dare? Because you shouldn't tempt me, I—'

He silenced her with a kiss.

'You do that a lot,' she murmured against the corner of his mouth when they finally came up for air.

'Do what?'

'Distract me with a kiss.'

'Does it work?'

She tapped her bottom lip, pretending to think. 'Not sure. You'll have to keep doing it so I can give you a fully researched answer.'

He laughed and slung an arm around her shoulder as they stepped into the Salus Per Aquum.

'Wow,' they both murmured at the same time, catching sight of the pool and spas.

Deep indigo and rich emerald shimmered off the tiled walls, a dark, tempting grotto that beckoned with its tranquillity.

'I'd like to get you alone in there,' he whispered against her hair, his arm tightening around her shoulders.

'Why? So you could give me another concussion like the last time we were in a pool together?'

'Just think of what came after the concussion.'

Excitement rippled along every nerve ending at the memory.

'I'm off to have this massage, then we'll work later.'

'Sure thing.'

His lingering kiss almost made her forget the all-important work part of later.

Impressed by his ability to consistently surprise her, she followed her therapist into a candlelit room where the woman proceeded to blend a lavender essential oil with a warm oil base and kneaded and stroked her body with masterful hands.

She should've relaxed at the perfect pressure, but

all she could think about was why Roman continued to distract her rather than answer her questions.

For a guy who was in this for the publicity, and who'd gone out of his way to help her secure this trial, he seemed strangely reluctant to actually sit down and get started.

She'd mentioned conducting the interview yesterday: he'd organised the scenic plane ride.

She'd pushed to do it today: he arranged this spontaneous massage.

She couldn't figure him out.

'You're very tense,' the therapist said, kneading her shoulders with a firmness she needed.

She wanted to respond with, 'You'd be tense too if you had a roguish charmer twisting you into knots.'

She settled for, 'Occupational hazard.'

'You spend time on a computer, right?'

'Yeah.'

And loved every second of it. She used to resent the hours spent in front of a PC screen number crunching. Now, over the last few days, she'd happily typed up her research on extreme sports and her interview questions and a whole host of other stuff just because it felt good.

'You need to relax to enjoy the full benefits of the massage.'

Okay, no more mental ruminating over Roman's motivations. But as soon as she'd finished here she'd bail him up and ensure he answered her questions.

If Roman had any more ideas to distract her, she'd remind him of her deadline.

And of the benefits of finishing work early.

The thought of those *benefits* turned her muscles to mush.

'That's better.'

She smiled, wondering what the therapist would think of her relaxation method and not particularly caring.

Roman's research portfolio was bursting at the seams. He'd discovered many new places around Australia to add to his employer's growing list of extreme-sporting hot spots around the world.

Towering cliff faces and challenging waterways he'd test run himself: scaling, climbing, jumping, wake-boarding, he'd packed in as much as he could into his fortnight here, travelling from South Australia across to Victoria and now here, Queensland.

With every jump, every twist, every leap, he'd obliterated that final confrontation with his mum.

He'd let adrenalin do the job of soothing him as it had always done, seeking escape in dizzying heights and bone-jarring speeds.

Now he had a different distraction in the form of a beautiful, intelligent woman who was slowly but surely creeping under his guard.

It was why he'd put off the interview so long.

It was why he was contemplating calling it off completely.

For if she'd succeeded in getting this close to him simply by spending time together, what would happen if she started delving?

He couldn't tell her about Estelle yet there was nothing surer than her asking about his family. Any good journo would. He'd fielded personal questions in the past by glossing over them or supplying a trite, superficial answer before following up with his next stunt to distract.

He had a feeling distraction wouldn't work with Ava.

She had a way of looking at him, as if she could see deep down beneath his gung-ho, adrenalin-addicted cowboy façade, as if she could see the real him.

And it scared him to death.

He knew calling off the interview was out of the question, when her potential new job depended on it.

He also knew he couldn't fob her off with any more distractions; there were only so many times she'd submit to a jump and massage.

Only one thing to do.

Mentally rehearse his answers.

Focus on his extreme sporting lifestyle.

Stay clear of personal stuff.

Stuff like how he'd berated himself for years over his mum's coping strategies, how he blamed himself for her condition.

Stuff like how maybe if he hadn't left home early to escape the nightmare, maybe she wouldn't be the way she was.

Stuff like how he continued to fall into her passive-aggressive trap, how he still wanted to help, how powerless he felt.

Over time he'd learned that no amount of self-recriminations or self-flagellating would change Estelle and he'd do better focusing his energies on being there when she needed him rather than lamenting a situation he couldn't change.

He'd often wondered whether having a dad around would've changed the outcome, whether Estelle would've been a different person.

As a kid, during his mum's worst bouts, he'd hide under the covers, squeeze his eyes shut and daydream of having a happy family like most of the kids at school. He'd dreamed of a mum who paid attention to him all the time, a mum who baked cookies and helped with his homework and attended his sports days.

He'd dreamed of a dad to wake-board with, a dad to speed ski with, a dad with the same daredevil streak he had.

When neither of those dreams came true he constructed a new dream, one where he was admired for his achievements, where people respected him, where they acknowledged him all the time and not only to lash out or play emotional games.

And he'd done everything in his power to make the last dream come true. Extreme sports had saved him, had given him a purpose, a focus and no way would he let his mother's threats ruin that.

Escaping to Australia might be a temporary solution but he hoped by the time he made it back to London she'd be out of her latest funk, the one that threatened to destroy him.

His phone beeped and he checked the text, his heart instantly lightening when he recognised Ava's number.

Doing more research before your interview.
Rain check on this afternoon.
C U 2nite?

Oh, she'd definitely see him tonight. Maybe he could distract her long enough to put off the interview another day?

His thumb hovered over the keypad while he composed a suitable response. When it came to him, his face eased into a grin.

2nite OK.
Looking forward to researching your other project, the erotica novel,
R XXX

He bet she'd get the triple-X reference and laugh.

Oh yeah, as far as he was concerned, tonight couldn't come quick enough.

Ava had no idea what Roman had in store tonight. The guy was just full of surprises and if last night was any indication it'd be something special.

Not that she needed the trappings. She'd be happy to curl up on the comfy couch in her room and order room service, as long as he was by her side. He made her laugh, he made her relax, he made her comfortable and for a girl who'd spent a lifetime feeling uncomfortable that was saying something.

Not that she could get too cosy. She had a few nights left and then their idyllic fling would be relegated to her memory, filed under 'incredible and unbelievable and unforgettable'.

And she wouldn't forget; Roman was that kind of guy. Besides, how could she forget the man who'd given her a part of herself back? A major part, if the genuine smiles and easy laughter were any indication.

When she'd smiled in her previous life, it had been for cameras or people watching. As for laughter, there hadn't been much in her dreary, fake life to laugh about.

Not that it had been all bad. She'd got along well with Leon, always had, but being good friends was no substitute for a passion-filled marriage some of her uni friends had chosen. If she could call them friends. She'd always wondered if people drifted to her because of her name and who she was.

Hell, she'd even thought that of Leon: had he married her to curry favour with her dad and his political party? Had she been a convenient, useful means to an end?

She'd asked him once, after a fine bottle of Shiraz, and he'd merely reiterated the reasons he'd given her when he proposed: they moved in the same circles, they were highly compatible, their families were close and their friendship was strong.

He'd said he loved her too and back then she'd thought it'd be enough. But she'd known all along his love had been more platonic than fireworks and like everything else in her life back then it was easier to go with the flow.

Where would she be now if Leon hadn't broached a separation? Would she still be trapped in a dead-end marriage and a mindless job, smiling on the outside while screaming on the inside wishing things could be different?

She liked to think she would've cracked eventually and blurted the unhappy truth to him but in reality she didn't have the guts.

Not like Roman. He had guts and determination and threw himself off high stuff in his spare time. He lived in the moment and embraced everything life offered. And for this brief interlude she'd become that person too.

She had so much to thank him for. But she didn't want to get all deep and meaningful. It wouldn't be his style and she'd vowed it wouldn't be hers for the limited time they had together. Besides, what could she say?

You changed my life.

You made me realise what I've been missing all these years.

You helped me discover what I want in a man.

If she took a chance on a relationship some time in the distant future. And she would. While her independence was all important now, there'd come a time ten years down the track, give or take a few years, when she'd be ready to risk her heart again.

Though had she really risked it to begin with? She certainly hadn't given her heart to Leon. Not in the same way she had with Roman.

She stopped dead and slammed her palm against the nearest wall for support as the realisation crashed over her.

She'd given her heart to Roman?

Impossible.

This thing between them was a fling, nothing more, nothing less.

Then why the sinking, leaden feeling in her chest that she'd gone ahead and done just that?

Dragging in a steadying breath, she glanced at her watch. Ten minutes late already.

She couldn't beg off tonight, not when she'd worked all afternoon; caught up in her article she'd missed dinner too and had called up a belated room service.

He'd been so great to her and made her promise to meet him at the front of the hotel at eight.

As much as she'd rather hide in her room where she could convince herself not the tiniest bit of her heart was involved, she had to face him and probably have the fact she'd fallen for him rubbed in.

Assuming the stoic mask she'd used to great effect when in long greeting lines, she took the final few steps to the monstrous glass entry doors, noticing Roman outside.

He had his back to her, giving her time to check out the way the faded denim clung to his butt, his long legs, his muscular shoulders encased in soft white cotton.

A small wistful sigh escaped her lips and as if he had supersonic hearing, he turned.

He eased into a smile as he caught sight of her and
her heart flipped.

Oh yeah, she was in way over her head with this one.

He held out his hand and she placed hers in his.

That was when her newly created world detonated.

CHAPTER NINE

Momentarily blinded by the flashes, Ava gripped Roman's hand like a life buoy.

She blinked, hoping every one of the paparazzi's stupid photos would be spoiled by her closed eyes.

Microphones thrust into her face and she leaned away, inadvertently stepping closer to Roman, who'd positioned himself on an angle to protect her.

'Okay, folks, settle down and we'll answer your questions.'

Her eyes snapped open at his proclamation. Answer intrusive questions from the vultures? Like hell.

She ignored the microphones waving in front of her face and glared at him, hoping to convey her distress with a glance.

To her shock, he had a confident grin on his face, as if he was lapping up the attention.

Right then, it hit her how different they were. He loved the adulation of a crowd, any crowd by the looks of it, while she couldn't get away quick enough.

With good reason, considering the hatchet job she'd recently weathered, but to see Roman with his shoulders squared and relaxed posture, seemingly beckoning the reporters closer, annoyed her more than their unexpected intrusion.

'Miss Beckett, is this your new man?'

'Is he the reason behind your recent divorce?'

'What does your father think about you flaunting a new romance so soon after your divorce?'

'Have you left Canberra for good?'

'Any comment to make?'

The questions peppered her from all angles and she shrank away, grateful when Roman released her hand to slide a protective arm around her waist.

'No comment for now,' he said, ushering her back into the hotel.

'We'll camp out here 'til she does give us one,' someone shouted and she inwardly shuddered.

How long had they camped outside her Canberra house following the divorce? Four whole days until she'd had a gutful of being a prisoner in her own home and had ventured out, mistakenly thinking that giving a statement would send them away.

How wrong she'd been.

It'd been like throwing a bone to a pack of rabid dogs and the frenzy that had ensued in every magazine and newspaper had been horrifying.

They'd twisted her words and had written vile things, had mistaken the reserved mask she'd presented to the world in the past for self-protection as an arrogant aloofness; said that she looked down on everyone not in her social circle.

While it had been lies, it had hurt. A lot. The sting only exacerbated by the angel they'd made Leon out to be. Not that she begrudged her ex his stellar standing in the press, but when they mistook his constant smiles and readiness to answer their questions as anything other than a politician doing his job, it rankled.

Now they'd found her and the horrible intrusion would start all over again.

Clamping her lips together to stop the sudden sob bubbling up from within, she allowed Roman to lead her towards the lift.

When he risked a glance her way she studiously ignored him, staring straight ahead, waiting for the urge to bawl to subside before she said anything.

Smart guy, he remained silent until they reached his room and he held the door open for her.

'I'm not staying.'

He frowned and shook his head. 'We need to talk in private, that's why I brought you here.'

Ashamed she'd allowed her anger to taint their conversation before it had begun, she swept past him, waiting until the door shut before turning to face him.

'Did you know about them?'

'By them I'm assuming you mean the paparazzi?'

She bit back her first response of, 'Don't play dumb with me.'

Antagonising him wouldn't be conducive to getting the answers she needed; and the interview she still needed for a shot at a freelancing job.

'Were they here for you?'

His eyes narrowed at her abrupt tone, the faint crease between his brows deepening. 'Looks like they weren't interested in me.'

'You didn't answer my question,' she snapped, the tenuous hold on her patience straining to breaking point.

'You're overwrought. Have a seat.'

He crossed his arms and propped against a table, his blasé act grating as much as his deliberately blank expression.

'Maybe I'm *overwrought* because I was just ambushed outside a hotel where no one supposedly knows me.'

'They won't be a problem—'

'They're going to camp out 'til they get a statement! Of course that's a problem.'

She hated sounding like an irate banshee, hated how this changed everything. Now she'd have to tell him about the smear campaign post-divorce, about her running away and why.

'We could just lay low for a while. Hide out in here.'

Her anger deflated, more from his use of 'we' than the complete logic of his statement. The guy was the epitome of cool. Did nothing ever faze him?

Collapsing into the nearest chair, she dragged a hand over her face. 'I'm sorry for acting like a crazy person.'

'You don't like the press. I get it.'

'Do you?'

'Yeah.' He pushed off the table he'd been propped on and took a seat next to her. 'You grew up in the spotlight. Being the PM's daughter must've been hell, having your every move scrutinised.'

And the rest. But she didn't want to talk about the rest and she nodded, content to let him believe that was the reason for her paranoia.

'Now that I've left that life I value my privacy even more and having them ask those ridiculous questions...'

She winced at the memory of them.

'Yet it's okay for you to ask me a whole host of questions, prying into my inner depths, analysing my answers, writing goodness knows what about me?'

She smiled as he intended, her heart kicking when he took her hand.

'I have no idea why the press are here, probably for

some VIP staying at the hotel and when they caught sight of you, they pounced.'

'You didn't seem averse to their presence?'

'That's because this face is meant to be plastered across media outlets.'

He turned his head side on, exaggerating his profile, and she laughed.

'Is there nothing you wouldn't do for publicity?'

He tensed, releasing her hand as he turned to face her, his eyes filled with an untold pain before he blinked and erased it.

'I'd draw the line at nudity.'

She held her hand up and pretended to write on it with an imaginary pen. 'Damn, scratch the first question off my list.'

'Speaking of questions, guess I should answer yours.'

He wanted to do the interview *now*?

After sidestepping for days he chose the oddest of times to turn professional. With her nerves frazzled and her head still ringing from those horrid questions, she'd rather hole up in her room for a while.

But Roman was right. With the press camped outside the hotel now they'd discovered her presence with a potential new angle to her supposed sordid life, best to hide away for the remaining time here. And the faster she completed this interview, the faster she found out whether she had a shot at doing this job for real.

She held up her hand with fingers outstretched. 'Give me five minutes to grab my stuff and I'll be back.'

'Unless you want to do it down in the lobby bar?'

A sliver of disappointment lodged in her heart. She'd hoped that after the interview they could switch to relaxation mode, that he'd wrap his arms around her and help obliterate the nasty discovery of having the paparazzi stalking her once again.

In fact, it was the first time they'd been together in his room that he hadn't wanted to jump her; which begged the question why?

'Sure, see you down there.'

She didn't wait for an answer. She didn't wait for an explanation. She'd been waiting her entire life to get where she was finally going and there was no way she'd jeopardise her plans now because her heart was taking a different track from her head.

Roman paced his suite for a good two minutes after Ava left, mentally rehashing the balls-up in his head.

How had his plans for a romantic evening ended in disaster?

He knew the exact moment the whole night had gone pear-shaped: when the press had bombarded Ava. What he didn't know was why.

Sure, he'd let her off the hook with his understanding of how tough life must've been as the PM's daughter, but he didn't buy it.

For someone used to being in the public eye, her reaction had been over the top. He'd expected her to assume a stoic mask, give them some trite answer and walk out of the hotel grounds with her head held high. What he hadn't expected was to see her freeze and clam up, as if she'd never had a microphone thrust in front of her face before.

He didn't get it.

Until the moment she freaked he'd been quite prepared to take the intrusion in his stride, to field a few questions, flash his usual smile for the cameras and continue about his business.

The funny thing was the press didn't have a clue to his identity. Ironic, when he'd been photographed the world over; albeit usually about to jump off a cliff or bridge. Then again, wasn't that the reason he'd chosen Australia as a break in the first place? A full twenty-four hours away from his mother and her threats. Threats he knew were fuelled by alcohol and melancholia but threats that could end his career all the same.

That was another reason he'd chosen Australia: he'd wanted Rex to run a great article on him as a pre-emptive strike against the potential damage Estelle could do just in case.

So here he was, finally about to give Ava the interview she wanted and feeling edgy because of it.

He'd used it as a distraction, wanted to divert her away from the whole 'is there nothing you wouldn't do for publicity?' thing she'd zoned in on.

He had his reasons for what he did, publicly or otherwise, and no way in hell would he be sharing those with anybody. Least of all a woman who had a talent for unerringly homing in on his deepest secrets and gently prodding them out of him.

It was why he'd suggested they meet downstairs for the interview: more formality, less intimacy. This suite held too many memories of the two of them entwined together, making desultory small talk, comfortable in a way he'd never been with any other woman.

When she started asking the hard questions he didn't want to be vulnerable, didn't want to run the risk of blurting what he feared most.

The next hour or two would be business. He'd stick to the facts and spin his usual rehearsed spiel to field her questions about family.

And once business was completed, well, they could

concentrate on the pleasure part of the evening, something he enjoyed much better.

It had taken Ava two hours to get the basic information she needed to write a decent article on Roman Gianakis.

He'd answered her warm-up questions quickly: the usual where was he born, was he sports-mad at school, how he got his start in the sport, followed up by how many extreme sports he participated in, what was his favourite, the next challenge.

She'd delved into his job as CEO for the extreme sports governing body, his role as ambassador for the sport and where he saw the future of the sports heading.

He'd given her in-depth, usable answers. Until she'd asked about family. He'd glossed over it, mentioning he'd rather keep his questionable paternity out of the article—perfectly understandable—and not elaborating on much else apart from he had no siblings and saw his mother in London on a regular basis.

There'd been no anecdotes, no smiles, no laid-back arm across the back of the chair, as for her previous questions. Uh-uh, he'd clammed up so tight she had a hard time prying anything further out of him when she moved on.

All she needed were a few more answers and she was done.

'You mentioned your home base is London at the moment. Do you spend a lot of time there?'

Once again his expression closed down and she pretended not to notice, focusing on her pen doodling on the edges of her notepad to keep from displaying the blatant curiosity burning her up inside.

'The bare minimum.'

Like his answers.

'If you weren't based there, where would you like to live?'

'Anywhere that has the highest cliffs, the roughest surf, the steepest ski slopes.'

A small sigh escaped her lips as somewhere deep inside twisted in disappointment. Practically, she knew this was a time-limited fling. Emotionally, she knew she'd moved way past that when she started to care about more than his superficialities.

'I'm always searching for the next big thing so where the toughest challenge is, I'll be there.'

The knife of disenchantment twisted further as she realised that was exactly how he might have viewed her: as a challenge, something to conquer before he moved on.

Her pen wobbled and she stabbed at the paper, making a great show of jotting notes. Out of necessity, for she knew if she stopped writing she'd be forced to look up to ask her next question and at that moment she couldn't face having her fears confirmed.

She'd known this from the start; they'd both spelled it out. But all the logic in the world couldn't ease the pain gripping her insides and squeezing hard.

That was when she knew she had to get away. Not away from the hotel, for she had the article to compile and needed to do that in complete privacy without the press messing with her head.

Away from him. She had to emotionally distance herself, for some time over the last few days her protected heart had failed to get the memo her head had dictated, the one that read 'fling only'.

She wanted to know about his family, wanted to know the *real* him, not for the article but for herself, for the woman at serious risk of falling for the wrong guy. If she hadn't already.

She didn't want his glib responses, she wanted the man who held her in his arms as if he'd never let go to open up to her.

In her lacklustre marriage she'd never had that, had never had real intimacy and the fact she'd felt so safe, so cherished in Roman's arms should've been warning enough she was in over her head.

She cared.

Much more than was good for her and the sooner she established space between them, the easier goodbye would be.

She snapped her notepad shut and thrust it into her bag, taking a composing breath before looking up and what she saw didn't reassure her one bit.

He was still wearing his 'public' face, the face he'd worn for the entire interview, a benevolent expression slashed with a winning smile every now and then. It was the face of a man who'd played to an audience countless times before, who knew all the moves, all the answers. And it was that expression as much as what he hadn't shared with her that gave her the impetus to surge to her feet.

'Thanks, I think I have all I need.'

'Great.'

He stood and reached for her but she made a great show of looking at her watch.

'Can't believe it's so late. I'm heading up to make a start—'

'Come back with me.'

He snagged her wrist and her pulse jackknifed.

A few hours ago, she would've liked nothing better than to be holed up in his suite, pretending the rest of today hadn't happened, as if they still had a blissful few days of no responsibility before their idyllic tryst ended.

But she was through pretending. She'd been pretending most of her life—pretending to be the model daughter, pretending to be happy in her life, pretending to be someone she wasn't—and she was done.

Forcing a smile, she shook her head. 'Sorry, I can't. You know how important this is to me. I only have a few days left and I really want to get this done.'

He dropped her wrist as if he'd been burned, his charming mask slipping for a second to reveal a fraction of the pain gnawing at her inside.

'Of course. You do what you have to do.'

They stood there like two strangers, stiff, awkward, unsure, the distance she craved already developing too quickly.

'Thanks, I'll see you later.'

He didn't say a word as she walked away, taking great care not to stumble on the highly polished exquisite marble.

It wasn't until the elevator doors slid shut and she'd sagged against the back wall did she allow her face to crumple.

Roman wasn't the only one proficient at keeping his inner self hidden behind a mask.

CHAPTER TEN

ROMAN stuck his surfboard in the sand and sank onto his towel, his mind blessedly clear as it usually was post-adrenalin rush.

Sadly, it didn't last long, as the thoughts he'd blissfully blocked out while riding monster waves crowded into his head, jostling for position.

It had been thirty-six hours since he'd seen Ava and she'd been all he could think about.

In that time he'd done three bungee jumps between windsurfing, powerboat racing, jet skiing, mountain biking, sandboarding and caving. He'd been up at the crack of dawn and fallen into bed when his body couldn't stand the frenetic pace any longer.

The adrenalin had helped but the moment he stopped the activities that never failed to soothe, Ava was in his head, whispering questions he had no desire to answer, questions that had him thinking about answers he'd rather not contemplate.

She'd got him thinking about Estelle too, about the choices he'd made, about changes that needed to be instigated if he wanted to maintain some kind of relationship with his mum.

She'd rung him late last night, had left a suitably

contrite, civil message, the usual thing she did following one of her binges.

How many times had he picked up the pieces for her? And how many times had she fallen down again, ignoring his advice and that of her doctor, preferring to submerge her sorrows in a bottle than face up to reality?

After her last outburst he'd said he was through. Her threats had hit home and he'd already given up too much over the years to allow her to tear down the professional reputation he'd carefully built.

This time he'd walked away.

Yet she'd called him again despite vowing not to. Not that he'd expected her to keep a promise when she'd reneged on the rest of her half-assed assurances when he was growing up.

How many times had she ranted and threatened and verbally abused? Too many to count yet he'd stood by her, helping her to regain equilibrium after each bout.

Now he was done.

He couldn't return her call, not now. He was still too mad, too hurt.

And that brought him back to Ava.

How the hell could he be hurting from not seeing her? He'd called her twice and while she'd been polite there'd been an invisible barrier between them whereas before there'd only been flirting and sizzle and laughter.

She had an important article to write, he got that. What he didn't understand was her aloofness, almost as if once she'd got what she wanted from him she didn't need him for much else.

Stupid, as she'd been as much into their fling as he'd been, but her hot and cold behaviour held shades of Estelle and he hated to compare her to his irresponsible, emotionally frigid mother.

A bunch of bikini-clad babes jogged past and he barely registered their coy smiles in his direction, which meant one of two things. Either he was seriously wiped out from catching those monsters waves or Ava had made more of an impact than he'd anticipated.

He didn't like feeling this…*uncertain.*

He knew what he wanted out of life and how to get it. He loved his life, every thrill-seeking second. He loved meeting people and schmoozing and being recognised. He loved the rush every time he skied faster or climbed higher or jumped quicker.

Yet right now his love of life had taken a dent, as if he were looking at everything through frosted glass. Where he'd had crystal-clear clarity before, everything was annoyingly fuzzy.

He didn't want to waste time determining Ava's motivation for pulling away when they still had a few days left. He'd vowed to never be the type of guy who second-guessed any decision he made. Yet feeling the way he did was firmly rooted in Ava's deliberate distancing and he was done mulling over why.

She'd had two days to whip the article into shape. Even if she hadn't finished it she'd have a decent first draft by now. Hadn't he mentioned something about proof-reading it before she submitted? If not, it was a damn good idea, an idea he'd have to present to her.

In person.

'What are you doing here?'

So much for the welcome Roman had hoped for. If Ava's abrupt tone hadn't clued him in, the fact she hadn't opened the door to her suite beyond a crack would've been a giveaway.

'I came to proof-read the article.' He tried a dazzling smile when she didn't budge. 'To give you my totally objective opinion, considering I'm the subject matter.'

'That makes you subjective.'

'Hair-splitting.'

His humour wasn't getting through to her and if he couldn't charm his way through the door, he was in serious trouble. It had never let him down before.

'I'd really like to help.'

She wavered for a moment, the door inching open before she drew her shoulders back and stared him down.

'Roman, I really need to work—'

'Bull. Just be honest with me.'

'You're a fine one to talk about honesty.'

A couple exited a room two doors down and gawked their way, and Ava flushed before flinging the door open and ushering him in. Nice. The risk of being embarrassed in public had succeeded where his charm had failed.

His memory receptors leapt as she brushed past him, the sexy bespoke fragrance of the Palazzo's toiletries clinging to her skin in an evocative veil, tempting him to bury his nose against her and inhale deeply.

'You want honesty? How about you start by telling me why you clammed up in that interview whenever your family was mentioned?'

Just like that, his erotic haze vanished.

'Only if you tell me why you've been avoiding me the last few days.'

She opened her mouth to respond and he held up a hand. 'And don't give me the work excuse, 'cause I get how important this article is to you, but I doubt you've been working on it non-stop for the last two days.'

Her eyes focused on the polished boards beneath her feet, unwilling to meet his gaze, though it was the slightest slump of her shoulders that had him broaching the distance between them.

She stiffened at his approach and he forced himself to keep his hands by his sides when all he wanted to do was touch her and hold her and reassure her that he was feeling just as confounded as her.

'Tell me, Ava.'

Her bottom lip quivered for a second and he clenched his fists to stop from bundling her into his arms, answers be damned.

Before he could think of something to say to retrieve this situation, she lifted her head and squared her shoulders.

'Was I just a challenge for you? The newest and brightest thing before you move on to the next?'

He swore and this time followed his instincts, crushing her to him. She resisted at first, her body stiff and unyielding but he didn't let go and after several seconds she relaxed into him.

'You know that's not how I think of you.'

He only just heard her muffled, 'How do I know?'

Gently disengaging, he held her at arm's length. 'Because we both felt that zing at the start, that special something drawing us together.'

He tilted her chin up and stared into her eyes. 'We've got an amazing chemistry and it was right there from the very beginning, surely you see that?'

Understanding scudded across her eyes as she reluctantly nodded.

'Is that why you've been keeping your distance?

Because you took one of my answers to your interview questions and twisted it around to second-guess yourself?'

She didn't need to answer; he saw all the affirmation he needed in her slight grimace.

Rubbing her upper arms, he said, 'Listen to me. You're a gorgeous, warm-hearted, incredible woman and I've had an unforgettable time.'

His stroking slowed as an answering spark lit her eyes. 'We don't have that much time left together. Let's make the most of it.'

Indecision warred with yearning before she deliberately looked away and he knew if he was to convince her he'd have to give her something more.

'You were right about me holding back. About my family.'

For the first time since he'd barged his way in here she touched him, a briefest brushing of her fingertips against the back of his hand, encouraging him to go on.

'You already know I haven't a clue about my dad.'

The urge to step back was strong but he forced his feet to stay. He'd finally made some inroads into getting Ava to listen; he'd be a fool to stuff it up now.

'And I think that's half the problem with my mum, the fact that whoever the guy was he's not around any more.'

He wished she'd say something but she remained silent, her attention unwavering. For a guy who usually lapped up this kind of attention, he found himself battling the urge to squirm. Then again, having the adulation and admiration following a jump was a hell of a lot easier to cope with than this intense one-on-one attention when he was semi-baring his soul.

'When I was a kid, my mum didn't want to know me.

She pretty much ignored me most of the time, which I hated. 'Til I started hating something else more.'

This time she slid her hand into his, intertwining her fingers through his before squeezing in reassurance.

'She had these really dark patches, where she'd hole up in her room for days. I learned not to intrude when she went ballistic once after I tried to bring her food.'

Acid burned his gut as he remembered the rest: the insults, the put-downs, the deliberate silences that went on for days. Ironic, in the end he'd come to prefer those fraught silences than her ranting.

'As I got older I realised those dark times were when she drank. Which didn't make sense, because I thought alcoholics craved a drink all the time but she'd be sober for a while then suddenly boom, she'd be hiding away with her stash.'

The gleam of tears in Ava's eyes slugged him as hard as his memories.

'I'm so sorry you had to grow up with that,' she said, holding his hand so tight it tingled.

He nodded his thanks, spooked by this urge to unburden himself but grateful if he had to talk about it that Ava was the listener.

'She's always had this inherent sadness that I attributed to not having my dad around, or maybe he broke her heart. Whatever the reason, her condition has worsened and these days she refuses help. The few stints in rehab have been a bust when she checks out after a day or two, she ignores medical advice...'

He choked off his 'and me' for it was pretty obvious from Estelle's sorry tale that her son had little influence in her life.

'What about you? Does she listen to you?'

His harsh laugh held little humour. 'I'm usually there to pick up the pieces but no, my opinion means little.'

'Have you tried—?'

'I've tried everything and now I'm done.'

She flinched as if he'd struck her. 'She's your mum, you can't abandon her—'

'She's threatened to ruin me, to take away the one thing she knows I've worked so hard for.'

Ava radiated pity and he hated it.

'My reputation is important to me, she knows that, and she said she'll plaster our sordid little family tale across the media.'

He wrenched his hand from hers and dragged it through his hair. 'Extreme sports is my life and I've spent years cultivating my reputation and it's helped get me to the top. I've got it all now. Fame. Recognition. Sponsors. Money. And the head-honcho job. But do you think she's happy for me?'

He shook his head, the pain of having his own mother want to ruin him slashing him anew.

'She wants to tear it all down, to turn the media I've learned to twist around my finger against me, unless I stop insisting on rehab.'

Ava laid a hand on his arm. 'She's only lashing out because she's frightened, terrified even.'

She wasn't the only one. Right now, with Ava touching him, listening to him, understanding him, he was terrified too, terrified of how she made him feel: as if he could tell her anything.

'I guess you're right. I'm the closest to her so I cop the brunt.'

Her hand slid down his forearm to clasp his. 'Has she made empty threats before?'

He shook his head, not wanting to relive their final confrontation even in his head. 'Nothing like this.'

'You're all she's got. She's probably afraid to lose you.'

It was as if a switch had flicked in his head and he stared at Ava in amazement. 'So you think she's trying to drive me away before I walk, that kind of thing?'

'Could be.'

She squeezed his hand for reassurance. 'If she refused to go to rehab and you've had enough of her binges, she must be petrified you're going to walk out of her life and never come back.'

'And the threat's a way of getting my attention and keeping me close.'

She nodded. 'She's your mother so she probably won't do it but either way you've got to confront this and sort it out.'

Feeling as if a weight had fallen from his shoulders, he glanced at the phone. 'She rang yesterday, left a civil message. I haven't returned her call.'

'Maybe you should?'

Ava released his hand and he immediately wanted to grab it back, to hold on to it for strength, for support, and that was when he realised how important she'd become to him.

No one knew about his mum. Not his sporting buddies, not his co-workers, not any of the women he dated.

Yet in less than a week Ava had crawled into his heart and curled up there, a niggling reminder that he wasn't as immune to emotional involvement as he'd always professed.

He cupped her cheek. 'Thanks.'

'For what? Speaking your thoughts out loud? I was just a sounding board—'

'For listening, for understanding.'

He wanted to kiss her so badly he ached but he reined in his impulse, knowing he'd shatter the tenuous bond they'd developed over the last few minutes with any overt displays of physicality.

Until now, that was all their relationship had been built on and it had suited him just fine. They'd be separating in a few days, their lives heading down different paths. So why the insistent, gnawing unease he'd be losing something precious?

She must've seen a spark in his eyes for she stepped away, his hand falling uselessly to his side.

'I really do have to work.'

Her rejection now, after he'd just unburdened himself for the first time to a woman, stung like hell.

'But maybe we can catch up later?'

The tension around his mouth eased into a smile. 'You're on.'

Unable to resist touching her one last time, he traced her deliciously tempting bottom lip with his thumb. 'Let me know when you're done, okay?'

Her tongue darted out to follow the path his thumb had just traversed and his groin tightened in response.

He had to get out of here.

'See you later.'

He'd almost made it out of the door when she said, 'Thanks for trusting me enough to share that stuff about your mum.'

With his hand on the door handle, his heart gave another uncharacteristic lurch and this time, he bolted.

Ava had run out of excuses to stay away from Roman.

She'd made a highly convincing list in her head the last few days: she had an important article to write, she had to research other jobs just in case Rex hated what she wrote, she had to start house-hunting on the Net, she had to protect herself from falling any deeper.

That last excuse had been the clincher and she'd buried herself in work, deciphering and collating the answers Roman had given her, merging them with the information she'd gleaned through research and presenting it in an interesting, informative article she hoped readers of *Globetrotter* would devour.

The good news, she'd finished the first draft.

The bad news, the moment she'd seen Roman again all her previous excuses had instantly wiped clean.

He'd opened up to her, really opened up, and that had meant more to her than all the toe-curling kisses and intimate caresses over the last week.

She understood him now: what drove him to seek out publicity. He craved attention he'd never got as a kid. As for valuing his reputation and wanting to protect it at all costs, she empathised one hundred per cent.

She'd worked a lifetime at cultivating an image her dad could be proud of, and later Leon. But her version of polite elegance she'd presented to the world had been misinterpreted and twisted to sell newspapers. What would the press that adored Roman do if they were fed sordid, elaborate tales by his mother?

Tonight, she didn't want to think about her past or his future. She had to make the most of their limited time left and with a determined step she pushed open the glass door to the Salus Per Aquum.

Once again the striking ambiance of the dark indigo and emerald pool made her blink, the darkness broken by a few muted down-lights. She'd never seen anything like this, the atmosphere a potent mix of decadent relaxation and exotic mystery.

Stepping onto the tiles, she glanced around for any sign of Roman when she heard the door lock click.

'Glad you could make it.'

She turned, her heart thudding painfully at the sight of him in the hotel's signature ebony plush bathrobe. He wore a wicked grin along with the robe and it catapulted her straight back to their first meeting.

Had it only been a few days ago? Could her life have changed so radically in that time frame? Logically, it didn't make sense. Then again, she'd spent her life being logical and methodical and look where that had got her.

Willing her pulse to subside, she waited as he stalked towards her, sinful and scintillating and sexy as hell in that robe.

'You work too hard.'

'If it means I get to unwind here, maybe it's worth it.'

'I'll make it worth your while, trust me.'

Her breath hitched a little as he took her hand and led her to the pool's edge, sliding his hands around her waist from behind and untying her sash.

Sensation rippled through her body as he slid the robe off her shoulders, revealing a simple black one-piece, the cross back being the only variation on the swimsuit she'd been wearing when they met.

Not remotely sexy but when his hand splayed against her belly and pulled her back against the evidence of how much he wanted her, she felt like the most beautiful woman in the world.

'You've got a thing for pools, don't you?'

'I've got a thing for you,' he whispered in her ear, shrugging off his robe before taking her hand and leading her into the water.

I've got a thing for you.

Each word shot like an arrow and lodged in the last place she needed: her heart.

He meant nothing by it. But hot on the heels of his opening up to her this afternoon it merely served to reinforce her treacherous position.

Given half a chance and a little longer she could easily fall in love with this guy.

Bad move. Seriously bad move.

He chose that moment to tilt her chin up and look into her eyes and in the few seconds it took for her to slide a familiar mask in place the depth of her feeling was clearly visible.

It registered. For his eyes widened and his lips compressed and the slightest dent grooved his brows.

'Last one in's a rotten egg.'

Releasing his hand, she dived into the cool water, staying submerged for as long as she could hold her breath, buying precious time to ensure she didn't make the same mistake again.

When she finally broke the surface he was right there, his hands spanning her waist as he lifted her up so she had no option but to wrap her legs around him.

'We're in a public place.'

'I booked out the Salus.'

'People do that?'

'I did it. For you,' he said, adding to her confusion.

By his reaction to her emotionally revealing slip-up, she would've thought he'd stick to slick lines and funny quips.

This intensity? Unexpected.

'Why?'

Capturing her face in his hands, he stared at her so seriously her lungs seized.

'The last few days have been great, Ava. Really great.

And I hope you know how memorable this time together has been.'

Now she knew where this was going.

Searching his dark eyes, as fathomless as the water lapping them, she came out with it.

'This is a goodbye speech, right?'

Regret clouded his face. 'I leave in the morning.'

'A day early.'

It was a statement, not a question and while she'd known this moment was inevitable it didn't make it any less painful.

'Some work in the Whitsundays has come my way.'

'Sure, I understand completely.'

Then she did what she'd always done when faced with unpleasantness: fixed a great big smile on her face and pretended it didn't mean a damn.

'I've had a great time too. Thanks for everything.'

She untangled her legs and pushed away from him, and he let her go.

She had no idea how he'd planned this evening to go but she had two choices: make an excuse and run or make the most of their last night together.

Jogging lightly up the steps, she grabbed her robe and slipped into it, tying the sash as she glanced over her shoulder.

She'd never forget this moment, with the man she had feelings for standing waist deep in shimmering midnight-blue water, looking like Neptune rising from the deep.

She couldn't read his expression in the dimness, but she bet it read relief she'd accepted his departure stoically.

He'd wait for her to make a move.

'If we only have tonight left, I'd rather spend it in your suite, so what are you waiting for?'

CHAPTER ELEVEN

ROMAN had taken the only way out.

Could also be construed as the coward's way out but he preferred to think of it as being smart. The instant he'd seen that look in Ava's eyes at the pool last night, he knew he had to get out. Fast.

For all her vows of independence and living in the moment and having a fling, he knew that look: the look of emotional involvement. The look of a woman who'd moved past their easy-going fling and into a no-go zone.

He never would've picked it, especially considering her history. Recently divorced women weren't usually in the market for a relationship. But Ava had certainly had that look in her eye last night and he'd done what he'd done his whole life: run.

She'd bought his business excuse but he'd seen the momentary hurt, quickly masked by her customary bravado. And rather than give him some flimsy excuse to avoid him for the rest of the night, she'd blown his mind with her pluck, issuing that challenge to make the most of their remaining time together.

They'd done that and how, but that was where he'd taken the coward's way out and done a runner. Him, who'd never shirked a bridge or cliff or building in his life? Who'd held the record for the highest altitude free-fall jump? Who'd challenge any fellow adventure-sport fanatic to climb higher or fall longer or ski faster?

He didn't avoid challenges, he faced them head-on, grabbing them with both hands and giving them a good shake along the way.

So what the hell had happened with Ava?

He could blame it on her getting too close. He could blame it on avoiding the dreaded goodbye. But deep down, he knew who to blame and he was looking at that guy in the jet's restroom mirror.

The truth was he'd felt something for Ava, had felt something for a woman for the first time in his life and he couldn't deal with it.

Coming clean to her about his mum might have been cathartic but it had cemented what he already suspected: falling for Ava would be far scarier than any jump he'd ever faced.

Everything else was supposition: her supposed depth of feelings for him, the possibility she'd want more after their fling. Excuses he'd fabricated to get a handle on what was really going on here: *he* had the feelings, *he* had the problem, *he'd* done the wrong thing.

He should've stayed and said a proper goodbye, not left that lame note in the early hours of the morning. Then again, what could he have said if he'd stuck around?

Thanks for a good time, see you round?

No, it was better this way.

Yet the longer he stared at himself in the mirror, saw disgust downturn his mouth and self-recrimination cloud his eyes, he knew he couldn't leave things like this.

She deserved more.

She deserved the world on a platter and then some.

Pity he couldn't be the guy to deliver it but for now he could do the right thing, the honourable thing, and ring her.

When he reached Hamilton Island, and figured out what the hell he'd say to make it up to her.

After everything she'd been through Ava was a realist.

She'd learned long ago dreams didn't always come true and it was best to make the most of what you had. So as she clutched Roman's crumpled note in her fist she knew the way he'd left was for the best.

Yet all the common sense in the world didn't make it any easier and to her horror a tear leaked from the corner of her eyes and trickled down her cheek, exacerbating her pity party for one.

Not that the note had been bad.

Thanks for a memorable time, Ava.
I'll never forget my Aussie adventure.
Follow your dreams.
Roman X

Was she crazy hanging on to that one little x? Lamenting the lack of 'love'? Shouldn't she be angry how he'd slunk out of here without saying a proper goodbye?

Crumpling the note into a tighter fist, she knew anger would be fruitless. She didn't blame him for leaving the way he had. She probably would've done the same thing, to avoid fumbling for words when the time came to leave. What could they say?

She'd had her answer to an unasked question last night when he'd cited business as a quick getaway after glimpsing an uncharacteristic show of emotion from her.

Crazy thing was, after the way he'd opened up to her about his mum she'd thought they might have a chance at something beyond a fling. Something real and tangible and sensational despite the roadblocks to a relationship: living on different continents, different lifestyles, different outlooks.

But beneath all that logic had been a glimmer of what if...*what if* she really cut loose and followed him around the world, seeking the next challenge, the next thrill? Would that be so bad? The beauty of freelance writing was she could do it anywhere and she knew, deep down, if Roman had asked her to go with him she would've.

But he hadn't and while her heart pined she was happy she'd taken what she could get. No regrets.

This was the new her, remember? No lingering in the past wishing things could be different. Now she had the power to make things different and she had every intention to, starting with putting the finishing touches on the article.

However, as she fired up her laptop she couldn't help but wish for an email, a phone call, something more than the note she'd carefully smoothed and pressed between the pages of her diary as a memento to an affair she'd never forget.

After working through the night, Ava hit the send button to Rex in the wee small hours, crossing her fingers and toes and anything else she could think of.

Thanks to Roman's generosity in extending her suite occupancy she didn't have to check out until tomorrow so rather than wallow in her room she'd chosen one of the hotel's poolside cabanas to relax and people watch.

Glamorous stick-thin women in designer bikinis swam alongside families happy to be in the warm Queensland sun, while attentive poolside waiters kept the cool drinks coming for those who wanted them.

She loved everything about this hotel, from the stunning marble interior to the thick, heavy black towels she now lay on.

As for those bespoke scented toiletries, she'd for ever associate the distinct fragrance with her time here and her time with Roman.

She squirmed around, trying to get comfortable, enjoying the semi-privacy afforded by the sheer material draped over her cabana creating the illusion of an Arabian four-poster bed, when her phone vibrated.

Hoping it'd be Rex and not recognising the private number on call display, she hit the answer button and put on her best phone voice.

'Ava Beckett speaking.'

'Sorry, must have the wrong number, I was hoping to speak to Ava Beck, the *Globetrotter*'s newest, bestest interviewer.'

Surprise and unexpected pleasure shimmied through her at the familiar deep timbre of Roman's voice.

'Shh, you'll give away my new identity.'

'Sweetheart, I'm on a veranda of a condo looking out over the ocean all by my lonesome so, trust me, no one's going to guess your secret.'

She could picture him, standing on the veranda of some upscale apartment in the Whitsundays, tanned and toned and incredibly gorgeous.

'Okay then, I guess my mystery identity is safe for now.'

She sounded so lame but what could she say?

I miss you.

I miss your smile and laugh and the way you used to drape your arm across my shoulders or guide me gently with a hand in the small of my back.

I miss your wicked sense of humour and the way your eyes darken to ebony when you're turned on.

I miss the way your adventurous streak rubs off on me and I want to be reckless for the first time in my life.

Sadly, she couldn't say any of those things. But she could ask why he'd called. Opting for honesty, she sat up straighter and clutched the phone to her ear.

'What's this call about?'

'Blunt as always—I like that.'

What she'd like was an answer. A guy who crept out in the early hours of the morning leaving a note didn't usually call the day after.

'I called to apologise.'

'For what?'

'Being a coward. Taking the easy way out.'

She didn't make him spell it out. They were past games.

'It was better that way.'

'No, it wasn't.'

She heard his sharp inhalation, the softest of exasperated sighs.

'I stuffed up. I thought it'd be easier leaving you like that, not having to prolong our goodbye, but I robbed us both of the opportunity to say what needed to be said.'

Resisting the urge to clutch her heart, she said, 'Like what?'

'Like how incredible our time together was. Like how we were great together. Like how...how cool it would've been if we'd had longer.'

He'd been about to say something else but she didn't push him, almost afraid of what he'd say. She hadn't expected him to be so honest and while her heart leapt for joy her rational brain knew it changed nothing.

'I really appreciate the call and you saying all that stuff.'

'Better than a crummy note, huh?'

'Aww...I don't know, there's something incredibly romantic about a note.'

He snorted. 'That's just the writer in you.'

She almost blurted 'Yeah, but you love me anyway' but thankfully had the foresight to bite back that particular clanger.

Not wanting to prolong the conversation in case she did say the wrong thing, she said, 'Well, thanks for the call.'

'Any time.'

Hating how awkward this was when they'd once sparred like pros, she opened her mouth to say goodbye when he rushed on.

'If you're ever in London, look me up.'

'Okay.'

'Take care.'

'You too.'

'Ava?'

'Yeah?'

'I miss you.'

He hung up before she could respond, leaving her staring at the phone and willing the ache in her heart to subside.

CHAPTER TWELVE

A CHAMPAGNE and several lemonades later, Ava still hadn't moved from her poolside cabana. She couldn't, for that would involve engaging her brain to do something other than ponder Roman's phone call and even now, half an hour later, she couldn't do it.

He'd called.

Guys who did a runner and left notes didn't call. They rode off into the sunset on their fictional Arabian stallions. But he'd called and she wasn't sure what surprised her more: the actual phone call or his 'I miss you' before hanging up.

Could those three little words mean they'd shared more than a fling? That he felt the same buzz beyond attraction that had zapped her out of the blue? If he did, what did it mean?

She had no idea if it was the scorching Main Beach sun or the champagne or the excessive mulling, but a blinder of a headache was building behind her eyes. Maybe a quick dip would clear her head?

As she dragged herself into a sitting position, the phone vibrated again and she tensed, her heart doing an expectant somersault.

With a shaky hand she grabbed the phone and

glanced at the screen, disappointed and excited and fearful when she saw Rex's number pop up.

What had she expected? For Roman to call back thirty minutes after his first call? That counted for the disappointment. As for the excitement and fear, Rex had called a few hours after she'd handed in the article.

The upside? She'd be put out of her misery sooner rather than later. The downside? If he hated her article she'd be left mooning over losing Roman and her fledgling writing career before it really began.

Crossing her fingers, she hit answer. 'Hi, Rex, good to hear from you.'

'Ava, glad I caught you.'

She could tell nothing from his bland tone and she squeezed her crossed fingers tighter.

'I've had a chance to read your article.'

'Great.'

Could she sound any more forced, fake and upbeat-perky if she tried?

'It's good, Ava. Really good.'

The breath she'd been holding whooshed out as she sank back against the cushions in a relieved huddle.

'So good in fact I'm sending you on an urgent mission, interviewing the owner of a new eco lodge. One of our regular contributors can't meet deadline and I need that slot filled asap.'

'Really?'

Cringing at how pathetically needy she sounded, she cleared her throat and tried again.

'I'm up for the challenge, thanks for the opportunity. Where will I be headed?'

'Hamilton Island.'

Her spine snapped upright as she clutched the phone to her ear. She didn't believe in coincidences. She believed in people using other people, people pulling strings to their advantage, people trying to get their own way by calling in favours behind the scenes.

Disillusionment pierced her excitement. She hadn't won this assignment on her merits. She'd been sent via the manipulations of a hotshot charmer who'd coerced his old family friend into doing his dirty work.

If he wanted to see her again he could've asked and the fact he'd done this made her want to thump him.

'By your silence, is there a problem?'

Hell yeah! But how to broach this delicately without losing her dream job in the process?

'Because I'd hoped you'd jump at this chance, Ava. Not many freelancers on trial get this kind of opportunity but your first article blew us away and we'd consider this Whitsunday Island piece your last trial so to speak. If you nail this, you're a bona fide *Globetrotter* employee.'

Ah, the double-edged sword. How many times had she heard someone approach her dad with a policy tweak or finance request or new tax levy, only to see him faced with the same dilemma she now faced?

If she stood up for her principles, she'd lose a golden opportunity and potentially her job. A hard-sought-after job she'd earned on her own.

Not because of whom she was.

Not because of her dad's name.

Just her. Ava.

Talented writer and proud of it.

The decision was a no-brainer. She'd save her anger for someone who deserved it and as soon as she got off this call she'd ring Roman.

'Thanks for the opportunity, Rex, you won't be disappointed.'

'Great. Your flight leaves tomorrow. I'll email you the details.'

'Fantastic. When's the deadline?'

'Week from today max.'

Not a problem. She could do the necessary research, interview the eco lodge owner, write the article and kick Roman's butt within seven days.

'I'll make sure you have it earlier.'

'That's what we like to hear. Look forward to reading it.'

'Thanks, Rex.'

The dial tone barely hummed in her ear before she found her recent call list and hit Roman's number.

She really, *really* hated that he'd taken the gloss off what should've been a great achievement.

She'd had so many doubts when she'd first got the opportunity to write but once the words had flowed her confidence had increased.

Now this.

He answered on the fifth ring and she dug her toes into the plush towel beneath her. Damn him. Even his voice had the power to curl her toes.

'How dare you interfere in my career again? You know how it bugged me first time around. Then you go and do this again. I thought—'

'Ava, slow down. What's wrong?'

'Like you don't know. Jeez, Roman, I thought you were different. I thought you respected me for who I was and—'

'Listen, I do respect you. And none of this is making sense. What do you think I've done?'

Just like that, she ran out of steam as embarrassment replaced her anger. She'd been so sure Roman had pulled strings with Rex again she hadn't stopped to think. Hurtling accusations was an ineffective interview technique. She would've done better taking time to calm down and rationally approach this rather than flying into a huff.

This really must be the new her because she never would've spoken to anyone the way she'd just spoken to him.

'Sorry for acting like a crazy person.'

'I'll forgive you if you tell me what this is all about.'

She heard the amusement in his tone and was grateful for it.

'Rex just called with my next assignment.'

Still unable to believe it, she said, 'I'm leaving for Hamilton Island tomorrow.'

'You're coming *here*?'

If she'd had any lingering doubts, he just cleared them up with his incredulous yell.

'Uh, yeah. I thought you may've had something to do with that?'

Gnawing on her bottom lip and feeling increasingly foolish, she added, 'You know, because Rex's an old friend of yours, maybe you pulled a few strings to get me assigned there like you did first time round.'

He chuckled and her toes dug in deeper.

'Sweetheart, I miss you a lot, but even I'm smart enough to know a guy doesn't get between an independent woman and her blossoming career, not after the way you bailed me up after the first time.'

'Okay then, guess I just made a total ass of myself—'

'But given time, basically another day of missing you, and I probably would've done what you accused me of.'

'You're missing me that much?' she scoffed, a tiny part of her wishing he'd say hell yeah.

'What do you think?'

His deliciously low voice reached into the deepest part of her, the yearning, craving part that missed him terribly, and plucked on her heartstrings.

'I think you owe me a tour of Hamilton Island to make up for having thoughts of potentially interfering in my career.'

'Hey! I'm not the one hurling wild accusations. I think you owe me. What are you going to do to make it up to me?'

Smiling at the realisation she'd be seeing him again so soon, she lowered her voice.

'Meet me for dinner my first night on the island and you'll find out.'

This time, she hung up on him.

Let him ponder while she processed the fact she'd be seeing the guy she'd fallen for again, on a spectacular Whitsunday Island, all in the name of work.

Next time she saw Rex maybe she should consider giving back her paycheque, for it seemed downright illegal to be getting paid for having this much fun.

Subduing an excited squeal, she swung her feet out of the cabana and gathered up her things. She had an email to check, packing to do and plans to make.

What *did* a girl wear to a romantic reunion dinner?

In all her travels, first with her dad and later Leon, she'd never visited the Whitsunday Islands.

A flying side trip to Cairns once during her dad's pre-election year but never the beautiful islands dotting the Pacific like pavlova crumbs on an indigo ceramic platter she'd seen from her window seat.

Flying economy on a commercial plane to far north Queensland hadn't been a patch on the jet she'd flown to Coolangatta, though she knew it had more to do with the absence of Roman than any lack on the airline's part.

That flight had been memorable; and also seemed like a lifetime ago. Had it only been early last week? How could she feel so close to Roman when she barely knew him? Though was time relevant? She'd known Leon most of her life yet had never experienced the same intimacy she'd had with Roman.

While she knew her trip to Hamilton Island would be fleeting, a week out of the rest of her life, she also knew seeing Roman again would cement what she already knew.

She'd quite possibly fallen a little bit in love with him.

She'd never felt like this before, never experienced the drop-away tummy, the hyperawareness of her body, the perpetual buzz making her eat less and smile more.

She should be glad she finally knew what love was, but could she have picked anyone less likely? They had absolutely zero chance of getting together, a fact she'd do well to remember when he tried to charm the pants off her.

And he would, she had no doubt, just as long as she didn't fall any deeper. Being a realist and acknowledging her feelings was one thing, believing in non-existent fairy tales another.

Roman was based in London, she'd be based wherever her job took her, if she was lucky enough to land a full-time position with *Globetrotter*.

Then why the sliver of sadness as she caught her first memorable glimpse of white sandy beaches, rocky cliffs, and a sparkling marina?

Crazy thing was, when the plane landed and she stepped out into the tropical heat, she searched the terminal for Roman, half fearing, half hoping he'd be here to meet her.

He wasn't but she spied a young guy in white shorts and navy polo holding a card with her name.

'Miss Beck?'

'That's me.'

Could she sound any dorkier? If she planned on using Beck as a pseudonym she'd better get used to it and not gawk at people when they called her.

'If you'll follow me, we'll be on our way.'

She handed over her bag when it appeared he wouldn't move until she did, and fell into step alongside him, quickly reaching the transport bays. Odd, she couldn't see any transport beyond a bunch of golf carts.

Confused, she stopped, and her chauffeur laughed. 'This is how we get around on the island. Hop in.'

Feeling as if she'd stepped from a seventies sitcom where guests landed on a fantasy island and were handed off into mobiles similar to these, she slid onto the seat beside him.

As the cart wound its way through leafy roads her driver kept up a steady commentary but all she could think about was how different this was from the cloistered rides she'd taken over the years. Rides in limos with their cool, darkened interiors and the heady expensive leathers, where she'd been told where to sit, when to keep her head lowered, when it was safe to step out flanked by obstreperous bodyguards. And she'd hated the partition separating the driver from the occupants, like some solid class divide.

Yet here she was, riding in the open air, not afraid to be seen, not afraid she'd be watched or criticised or chastened.

She grinned, relaxing against the seat, watching the

beautiful vista unfold around her. No place did verdant green foliage and cerulean oceans and pristine beaches like north Queensland and the fact she was here to work was still a tad on the pinch-worthy side.

The cart slowed after five minutes of steady climbing and pulled over into a natural garage made from overhanging rock.

Confused, she glanced around for a hotel.

'This is where you get out. Follow the path to the right. Mr Gianakis is waiting for you.'

She should've known. High-handed, confident and challenging, he'd commandeered her arrival here the same way he'd commandeered her heart.

'Uh, okay, thanks.'

Uncertain what to do with her bag and hoping the driver's version of 'a little way' wasn't a hike, she glanced around, indecisive.

'Your bags will be taken care of, miss.'

His tone implied 'don't keep the man waiting' and she nodded, muttered 'thanks' and stepped out, the warm breeze blowing her skirt around her legs. If she'd known Roman had intended to meet her on top of some great rock she wouldn't have worn a summer dress and espadrilles.

However, she'd barely taken ten steps along a well-worn track when she caught sight of him, standing on an outcrop, wind ruffling his dark hair off his neck, moulding his ivory shirt to his chest.

Her fingers ached to take a photo, to capture his magnificence as a still-shot. How many times would she look back on a photo like this in the future and wish he would be as captivated by her as he was for the view from that height?

He half turned, caught sight of her and the potency of his smile buffeted her almost clear off the mountain.

She ran.

An impulsive, spontaneous, completely corny gesture but she couldn't stop her feet any more than she could stop her feelings for him, and as she flung herself into his open arms and he spun her around and around she didn't regret it.

Whatever happened, she'd never regret opening her heart to this man. Regret was for bitter people dwelling on the past. And she wasn't that person. Not any more.

She squealed as the wind lifted her skirt and, laughing, he slowed, her body sliding against his until her feet touched the ground.

'I can't believe you're here,' he said, capturing her face between his hands, staring at her in wonder and awe.

'I can't believe you hired some guy in a golf buggy to bring me up here.'

He grinned and her muscles spasmed with want. 'I doubt you would've come on my preferred mode of transport.'

'Which is?'

He jerked his thumb over his left shoulder and she peered in that direction, seeing nothing.

'A little to the left.'

He guided her with his hands on her waist and she found it increasingly difficult to focus with them there.

'Oh no...' She caught sight of a great hulking black beast of a bike. With *two* helmets hanging off the handlebars. 'You're not expecting me to ride that thing back down the mountain, are you?'

He shrugged, the wicked glint in his eyes ensuring she'd have little option.

'There's always the other way I prefer.'

'Which is?'

'Parachuting off.'

She took one glance at the sheer drop off the cliff and jabbed him in the chest.

'Don't joke about stuff like that.'

He chuckled. 'You've already done a tandem jump so what's a little cliff jump between friends?'

'No.' She laid a palm against his chest. Any excuse. 'Way.'

'In that case, the bike it is.'

'I'll take the buggy, thanks.'

Sheepish, he shrugged. 'I gave Terry instructions to drop you off and not stick around.'

'You didn't!'

'I did.'

Tilting her chin up, she glared. 'Did anyone ever tell you you're pushy and presumptuous and—?'

His kiss stifled the rest of what she'd been about to say; whatever it was. She forgot the moment his lips touched hers. She forgot everything but the taste of him and the feel of him and the heat of him, setting her alight, encouraging her receptors to remember the many ways he'd pleasured her with these talented lips.

She clung to him, lost on a wave of sensation so powerful he could've slipped a parachute on her and she wouldn't have noticed, lost to everything but him.

She hadn't fallen just a little in love with him.

She'd fallen the whole damn way.

She'd eventually have to fathom a solution to this problem. For now, she was content for him to kiss her 'til sunset.

CHAPTER THIRTEEN

Ever since Roman heard Ava would be arriving on Hamilton Island he hadn't been thinking straight.

Work? His concentration was shot.

Dinner with old friends? He'd been caught daydreaming twice.

Play? In the past wakeboarding had always cleared his head; the rush of being dragged behind a boat, the spray in his face, the increasing speed. He'd tried three times and nothing, not a hint of a buzz.

He'd known then he was in serious trouble.

Extreme sports had never let him down. When he was dealing with his mother's indifference and subtle passive-aggressiveness and binges all those years, the adrenalin rush had been the one constant he could rely on.

Not getting that buzz this time scared him.

What if his addiction to Ava had replaced his adrenalin addiction?

The way he was feeling now, out of control, couldn't stop thinking about her, needing to see her desperately, it sure felt like an addiction.

He'd come here, the highest point of the island, to think, to strategise. When he was up high, whether it be on a plane about to jump or perched on a cliff, he felt invincible. As if he could do anything. Face any battle and come out on top. King of the world.

He'd assumed meeting Ava up here would give him clarity. It had only been a few days but he'd been going crazy without her, missing her with a staggering fierceness. He'd blurted some of what he was feeling on the phone when she'd rung accusing him of arranging her trip. Funnily enough, he probably would've done exactly that given a few more days of this uncharacteristic madness.

Now she was here and all his plans to romance her flew straight off the precipice. He couldn't keep his hands off her. And he couldn't keep his mind off anything but figuring out how he could keep her in his life longer than a week.

He had a few ideas but he needed to decipher them, rationalise them, before doing what he'd never done before: lay it on the line with a woman.

But the moment they'd kissed he'd known he couldn't wait and all the thinking in the world wouldn't change what he knew deep down: that she gave him a better buzz than any jump or dive or glide.

'Wow, you have missed me,' she said, touching her fingers to her lips, her eyes wide and shining and reflecting the perfect blue of the sky.

'You could say that.'

Her smile faded at his serious tone and he kicked himself for what he was about to lump on her when she'd only just arrived.

He had no choice. If he waited he knew this thing for her would continue eating at him and who knew what he'd blurt and when?

'What's up?'

'I've been doing a lot of thinking.'

Wariness replaced the excitement in her eyes. 'About?'

'Us.'

'Didn't know there was an us?'

Her emotionless voice scared him as much as the speed in which she deliberately blanked all expression.

He imagined she'd had loads of practice at assuming this careful mask, to show the world she didn't care. He knew why she was doing it now. She was scared too, scared what had started out as a lighthearted fling had developed into so much more.

Neither of them had expected this but it had happened anyway. Surely they owed it to themselves to give it a shot?

He took hold of her hands, noting the slight tremble in hers matched the tingle in his he usually got pre-jump.

'Let's not pretend, Ava. A fling was nice in theory but I think we both know the practice has evolved into something else.'

Her teeth worried her bottom lip. 'Like?'

'Like something deeper, something that won't go away.'

Squeezing her hands, he drew her closer. 'I can't stop thinking about you. What about you?'

'I can't stop thinking about me either.'

He laughed, loving her ability to break the tension. But her amusement faded quickly as she slid a hand out of his to reach up and cup his cheek.

'Same here.'

Her gaze dropped to focus on his chest. 'I've never felt this way about any guy before.'

Elation made him want to fist-pump the air. An elation that quickly deflated when she raised her eyes to meet his and he saw the rejection there before they'd even begun.

'But I've sacrificed too much for too long. I'm not willing to give it up for a relationship.'

'Who said anything about giving it up?'

Releasing her hands and taking a step back, he looked out over the island, trying to get his words straight.

'Long distance won't work,' she said, her finality chilling.

'I wasn't thinking long distance.'

He paced, before swivelling to face her, desperate to make her understand the convoluted thoughts twisting his brain into a pretzel.

'I talked to my mum and you were right. She's terrified I'll walk away and not look back, so she's been pushing me away deliberately.'

He drew in a deep breath, beyond grateful this incredibly insightful woman had helped him see sense where Estelle was concerned.

'She's promised to give rehab a serious go this time, along with AA after she comes out, as long as I'm there to support her so I'm stuck in London for however long it takes.'

The dampness in her eyes made them shine brighter than the ocean backdrop. 'That's great, for both of you.'

Hoping she'd go for the rest of his plan, he rushed on. 'So I was thinking what if you're based in London but continue to travel as widely as you need? You can still write for *Globetrotter*, maybe expand your portfolio and write for other European mags. But the thing is, you can always come back to London.

'To me,' he added, sounding like a dolt. As if she hadn't already understood that part.

He'd seen her tentative, he'd seen her aroused, he'd never seen her in open-mouthed shock.

'Not exactly the reaction I was hoping for,' he muttered, resuming his pacing, wishing she'd say something before he jumped off the cliff sans parachute.

'I can't believe this.'

She shook her head, as if the arrangement he'd just proposed was as out of reach as joining him on his next cliff dive.

'Look, forget I said anything—'

'I damn well won't.'

She grabbed at his arm, forcing him to stop. 'I can't believe you want to have a relationship. I can't believe you'd be happy to fit in around my career. I can't believe...'

'What?'

When she raised her eyes to his, she didn't have to say the words. The depth of emotion mirrored what he felt, but he'd bet she'd be much more eloquent expressing it.

'I can't believe we're going to give this a go.'

He let out a whoop and crushed her in his arms. Where he hoped she'd stay. For a very long time.

Like for ever.

Considering the staidness of her previous life, Ava had never been on a motorbike. Hadn't even been close to one. As she adjusted the chin strap on her helmet and wrapped her arms around Roman's waist she thought, *How hard can it be?*

Roman let rip a full throttle and eased the bike around, coasting onto the track leading down the mountain.

See? Nothing to worry about. Then the thing started

moving, seriously moving, and she screamed inside her visor.

Not that Roman drove particularly fast but with his offer of a relationship still sinking in, plus the altitude and curves and headiness of having her body plastered against his, she couldn't breathe.

The beautiful scenery was lost on her as she kept her eyes firmly shut for most of the ride and when the bike eventually slowed before stopping, she couldn't have moved if she tried. Her entire body felt stiff but surprisingly she felt the same buzz she'd had after the tandem jump: as if she could take on the world and conquer it.

Roman dismounted, shucked up his visor and helped her off. Lucky, for her legs had serious wobbles.

'Enjoy that?'

'Laugh a minute,' she said, reluctantly joining in his chuckles at her dry response.

'I love the way you embrace new experiences,' he said, helping her unstrap the helmet and slip it off.

She was past caring about her hair. With that descent down the mountain, it was probably standing on end anyway.

'And I love—how I feel when I'm with you.'

If he noticed her hesitation he didn't say anything, but the softness around his mouth and the twinkle in his eyes told her he knew what she'd been about to say and felt the same way.

A relationship. With this guy. In London. While she followed a new career path.

Could life get any better?

As they held hands and traversed the lobby of what she assumed was his hotel, or hers, it didn't matter as long as they made it to a room fast, she caught sight of a newsstand filled with magazines.

With her picture on the front.

She stumbled and Roman's grip tightened. 'You okay?'

Ice trickled through her veins and she shivered, wanting to look away but irrevocably drawn to impending disaster.

'Ava, honey, you're scaring me.'

Her lips moved but no sound came out, the horror of a month ago rushing back to swamp her in a sickening wave.

'Come over here, sit down—'

'No!'

Finding the strength to drag her gaze away from the visual nightmare she'd just walked into, she shook her head.

'I don't want to sit down...those magazines...'

Confusion clouded his eyes before he glanced across at the newsstand and bewilderment gave way to concern.

'Is that—?'

'Yep, that's me.'

Now the shock was wearing off and, increasingly incensed, she marched over to the newsstand, rummaged in her bag and handed over a wad of money, grabbing as many of the offending magazines as she could.

Unable to carry them all, she thrust half at Roman, who took them without a word. She'd seen his face wear many expressions: from roguish to amused, passionate to teasing. Never had she seen him like this: stricken, floundering, worried.

'I'm assuming this is your hotel?'

He nodded.

'Good, let's go talk in your room.'

'Ava, they're just dumb magazines—'

'Unless you want me to have a mini-meltdown right here I suggest we discuss this in private.'

His lips clamped shut and with one last concerned glance her way he headed for the lifts. Thankfully, he didn't speak and, clutching the offending magazines to her chest, she followed him into the lift.

As it moved the horror of her past swam up, a host of unwelcome memories.

Was she wearing a see-through skirt?

Was there spinach in her teeth?

Was the distance between her and her partner appropriate and unlikely to be misconstrued?

And that was before the nightmare of the divorce, spread across the tabloids for all to speculate.

Biting back the urge to scream, she marched down a corridor alongside Roman, the magazines in her arms weighing a ton, their content weighing on her conscience more.

She didn't have to open them to know what kind of rubbish had been written about her.

PM's daughter shacked up in Gold Coast love nest.

Ava Beckett under extreme heat with new lover.

From one extreme to another: PM's daughter runs from diplomat's arms into adrenalin junkie's.

Blah, blah, blah.

Roman unlocked his door in record time and she stomped in, knowing she'd have to get a handle on her temper before she said something stupid.

This wasn't his fault but a small part of her blamed him: for tempting her into a fling in the first place, for cultivating a relationship with the very vultures that'd written this rubbish about her. Irrational reasons fuelled by anger and exacerbating the emotions whirring through her like a pinwheel.

Having Roman propose a relationship had thrown her and having to cope with this hot on the heels of his heartfelt declaration…

He dumped his magazines on a glass table and she did the same, her gaze lighting on the top one, with an old pic of her taken last year at some garden tea party and the headline SUN, SEX & SIZZLE: PM'S DAUGHTER GOES TO EXTREMES.

Compressing her lips to stop from swearing, she picked it up and flicked through, her fury exponentially growing as she speed-read the drivel they'd written about her and Roman.

That was when it hit her.

Roman's precious reputation…

He'd walked away from his mother when she'd threatened to ruin it via the very medium she held in her trembling hands.

Oh no…

The magazine tumbled from her lifeless fingers as the implication sank through the numbness perforating her heart.

If they stayed together, his reputation wouldn't just be in jeopardy, it'd be ruined.

All the years of hard work he'd put into cultivating it, gone, torn to shreds, because of *her*.

She couldn't do it to him.

'Hey, sit down, you're shaking.'

He guided her into a nearby chair and she let him hold her, knowing it would be the last time.

'You know I'm going to throw all of these into the bin, right?'

She mumbled a response, her mind reeling at what she had to do. Tear apart their short-lived happiness and dreams of a future.

'They've probably invented a whole lot when they couldn't get a comment from us at the Palazzo so don't worry about it.'

She pulled out of his embrace, hating what she was about to do.

'Don't worry? Are you nuts?'

He winced. 'You're seriously peed off.'

'I passed seriously peed off about five minutes ago when I realised I can never escape this.'

Sharp regret, deep and cutting, slashed her resolve. But she loved him too much for him to lose everything because of her.

'As long as I'm with you.'

He flinched as if she'd struck him. 'Look, I know you hate the paparazzi because of your past but—'

'You know nothing about my past!'

Aching from the realisation she'd have to push him away once and for all, she lashed out, emotionally careening out of control.

'You want to know about my past? Try being a teenage girl having a bunch of sleazy PR guys watching what you eat and how much you exercise just because they think you're a few pounds too heavy for the cameras. Try having a homeless guy spit in your face because he thinks your dad's policies keep him on the streets. Try having some psycho creep stalk you because he has grand kidnapping plans to make a quick million.'

Her chest heaved as a red haze settled over her eyes. 'Try having a dad who only saw you as a prop, an adjunct to his all-important career. Try having bodyguards watching your every move on a trip to the mall so you can't even pee in peace. Try having a battered self-esteem because you have no idea whether people like you for who you are and not just your name.'

He reached out and she sidestepped him. 'Try having your divorce spread over the tabloids every day for a week. Having your character questioned and speculated over and found lacking. Being called everything from ice queen to frigid. Having people point at you in the street and snigger and worse. People who don't care about shredding your reputation...I can't do it.'

She tasted saltiness, unaware she'd started crying during her tirade and this time when he made a move to touch her she let him. She let him hold her. She let him smooth her back. She let him murmur comforting words.

Then she let him go.

Drained, she propped on the back of the couch, knowing if she sank into it she'd be tempted to not get back up.

'We can handle this—'

'No, we can't.'

She clutched the couch for support, her bravado wavering beneath the intensity of his bewildered hurt.

'You said it yourself, Roman. You're a celebrity. Your profile is important to you—you need publicity.'

'Extreme sports are underrated, I need to foster the right image for sponsors, competitions—'

'I understand but I can't do this again.'

'I'll be with you every step of the way, supporting you. We can travel to places anonymously, out-of-the-way places—'

'I don't want that kind of life.'

It ripped her heart to say it but she had to, had to make him understand the cost she was willing to pay for him.

'I don't want to hide away any more. I'm done skulking around because of the intrusion of others. I'm done ducking from long-range cameras and wearing stupid disguises. I'm done...'

He dragged in a breath, harsh in the gloomy silence.

'Where does that leave us?'

Regret clogged her throat, the burn of tears making her blink.

'I can't live under a spotlight again, Roman.'

The tears finally fell and she swiped them away. 'Even for you.'

His anguish matched hers as she strode towards the door and out of his life.

CHAPTER FOURTEEN

Ava interviewed the eco lodge owner, wrote her article and handed it in a day before deadline.

With her board paid until tomorrow she spent the day touring the island, swimming, trying to obliterate the memory of Roman now she'd stopped working.

But no matter how many laps she did or how many shops she browsed, she couldn't stop thinking about him. Thinking about the carefree, adventurous life he'd painted for both of them, with him following his dream of bringing his sport to the world's attention, her following her dream to write, to travel, to revel in her independence and the life she'd created for herself.

Oh yeah, she'd pondered it at great length but every time her fantasy life materialised in her head it disappeared just as quickly under the weight of flashing cameras and intrusive microphones and long-range lenses.

How many years had she put up with this? Too many but crazily she'd do it again if it meant Roman wouldn't be tarnished with her poor press reputation.

And that was what kept her away despite the constant urge to pick up the phone or visit his hotel. She knew he was still here; she'd seen flyers around advertising extreme sports tutoring with his handsome face beside the fine print and if she didn't love him so much she would've signed up for a crash course in whatever mad stunt he was teaching.

Logically, she was trying to protect him but her aching heart was having a hard time adjusting.

She'd been desperate for adventure a few weeks ago: new job, fresh start and he'd seemed like the perfect adjunct to that. Nothing serious, a bit of lighthearted fun, a transient guy with a nomad life who'd bring a taste of the illicit into her previously dull life.

Yet somewhere along the way her heart had opened to a gorgeous, warm-hearted, free-spirited, charming guy who had offered her a relationship with no strings attached.

And she'd sacrificed the lot for him.

Wrapping her arms around her middle, she hugged tight to stop the empty, sick feeling churning her belly.

Some day this pain would subside. For now she had to concentrate on rebuilding her life and forget how much she loved Roman and how much she'd lost for that love.

Roman snuck a peek behind the curtain into the hotel's ballroom and rubbed his hands together. Full house. Good, the more the merrier for what he had to say.

The irony wasn't lost on him; the paparazzi he'd deliberately cultivated in his career had ended up costing him the woman he loved.

Loved…

He still couldn't believe it. He loved Ava, a revelation that had been born of his misery and soul-searching the last week, leaving him tight-chested and confused and just a little bit crazy.

Over the last seven days he'd nursed his bruised ego, inventing all sorts of reasons why they wouldn't have worked and he'd be better off without her. Stupid, irrational reasons, such as they were too different and she'd never stick around now she'd found her independence and she was probably just on the rebound.

But for every lousy reason his head came up with, his heart counteracted with another: she was funny and smart and willing to expand her horizons. She was beautiful and caring and so cute in her quest to live in the moment.

He'd left her alone though, having no experience in chasing women and not wanting to start now. Yeah, he sounded like an arrogant jerk but it wasn't until a full week had passed he realised that was part of his problem.

Not the arrogance thing, but the fact he'd never had to work hard for female attention. His lifestyle, along with the danger aspect of his profession, ensured he was never short of female company. And he'd lapped it up, the same way he'd revelled in the adulation he'd received for his sporting prowess. Which made him think...was the attention as much of a buzz as the adrenalin rush?

Considering his mum had never paid him any—other than to make his life hell for 'holding her back'—it was probably all very Freudian. He wanted what he'd never got as a child. So where did all the psychoanalysis leave him?

Ava didn't want any part of the attention he lapped up. How could the two of them stand a chance when he needed to promote the celebrity status she abhorred?

He'd rehashed her final meltdown a hundred times in his head until he'd had a breakthrough. Something she'd said at the end about the press shredding reputations and it was as if a light bulb had gone off.

She'd said she didn't want to be part of his life because of his celebrity status but what if there was more to it? What if she'd taken all that stuff he'd blurted about his mum and his reputation, and was doing this out of some warped way to protect *him*?

He could imagine her doing something like that, something so self-sacrificing, just as she'd done her entire life. Giving up who she was, what she really wanted to be, to do right by her dad and her husband. What if this time round she was doing the same thing for him?

The more he thought about it, the stronger his gut latched onto it as the truth.

There was only one way to find out and that was why he'd called a press conference here today. Once Ava heard what he had to say he hoped the truth would set them free.

Hoping she'd come, he scanned the crowd, finally spotting her in the far back corner, hiding behind sunglasses shading half her face and a floppy straw hat, and his heart stopped. She'd achieved what no amount of sand-boarding or sky surfing or white-water kayaking had achieved. His heart had to have stopped because he couldn't breathe and it wasn't until he searched the crowd and found her again did it kick-start.

While his lungs did their best to inject oxygen into his bloodstream again, he drank in another glance at her, dragged in several deep breaths and kinked his neck from side to side in his usual warm-up ritual.

He rarely experienced more than a fizz of fear jumping out of a plane but stepping onto this stage and declaring the truth for the woman he loved in the hope she'd take him back?

Absolutely freaking terrifying.

* * *

When Ava had received an email from Rex saying she'd got the job, she'd been ecstatic. Until she read the addendum: she had to attend a press conference today to get the low-down on whatever announcement the hotel was making and possibly nab an interview with the owner.

She would've rather taken out a full-page ad in a major newspaper and posed naked than attend a room full of press but considering this was her first bonafide writing gig she had little choice.

Waiting 'til most of the crowd were inside, she slunk behind them, positioning herself against the farthest back corner. The sunglasses and hat were a little extreme but the last thing she needed was any of this crowd twigging to her identity.

A lone figure strode onto the stage and she sagged against the wall in shock.

Roman stared directly at her, his gaze defiant? Challenging? What was he trying to tell her? Better yet, what the hell was he doing up on stage?

Her confusion increased when he stepped up to the microphone, slid it out of its holder and brought it to his lips, not too close, not too far, a veteran.

'Thanks for coming today, ladies and gentleman. I promised you an exclusive and you're going to get it.'

Trepidation tiptoed across the back of her neck, raising hackles. She didn't like surprises and seeing the guy she loved in front of a crowd of jackals she usually despised? Didn't bode well.

They would've seen the articles written about him in conjunction with her: the supposition, the speculation. Surely he didn't want to be questioned less than a week after those trashy magazines had hit newsstands here?

'I called you here today because there have been a

lot of falsities reported and I want to clarify a few issues.'

Silence reigned and she stifled the urge to clear her throat.

'My life has been an open book for the press. I like you guys.'

He made a gun with his thumb and forefinger and cocked it at the audience, who laughed.

'But I don't like reading rubbish bordering on slander and that's what's been happening lately with a friend of mine.'

Her heart twanged. She'd been relegated to friend status. Considering how she'd walked away from his offer, she should be grateful.

'Though that's not entirely true. She's much more than a friend.'

His steely stare pinned her with a ferocity that snatched her breath.

'She's the woman I love.'

His gaze didn't waver and a few of the reporters started looking around, trying to follow his line of sight, while she shrank farther into the corner.

Why was he doing this? It could only hurt his reputation more than she already had.

'The thing is, she loves me too and has this warped way of showing it, by wanting to leave me in order to protect me.'

Shock ripped through her and she straightened, wishing she could read his expression from this distance. Had he really figured it out? Why she'd walked away from him?

'You see, my reputation is important to me. I've projected a certain image for a long time now but it's time to clue you in on the rest.'

Ava had no idea what Roman was about to say but the expectant silence pulsated with curiosity as the horde leaned forward collectively, waiting for their next titbit to blow up out of all proportion.

'My father? No idea who he was as my mum won't tell me but that's the least of her problems. She's an alcoholic who has finally agreed to go into rehab. And has given me the okay to tell you all of this.'

Not comprehending what brought on Roman's lapse into the full-blown truth, she struggled not to squirm under the impact of his unwavering stare. It was as if the room were empty and he were speaking directly to her.

'I wanted this all out in the open so there's absolutely no dirt you can dig up on me, nothing you can invent because now you know it all. And to my beautiful girlfriend who I love very much and who has been protecting me and my precious reputation, you have no excuse to not spend the rest of your life with me any more.'

The women in the crowd sighed and Ava blinked back tears.

He knew.

And he'd done all this for her. Stood up in front of this room, which equated the world once the copy hit their editors' desks, and laid bare his soul without thought for the reputation he'd spent a lifetime building.

If he loved her that much, and she loved him more, what was she waiting for?

She slid the sunglasses off, yanked off the hat and stuffed them into her bag, which she hid behind an indoor pot plant before squaring her shoulders and marching through the crowd towards the stage.

If Roman had done this for her, the least she could do was confront her demons for him.

Roman had been about to step off the stage when he saw Ava weaving her way through the crowd, cool and elegant in a calf-length lemon dress that skimmed her curves and accentuated the tan she'd acquired. She looked fresh and vibrant and ready to take on the world. His world with a bit of luck.

He'd laid his heart on the line but the closer she got to the stage he was no closer to determining whether she'd give them another chance.

Her heels clacked against the stairs as she stepped up onto the stage and the low buzz in the room died out to nothing.

He wanted to hug her, to kiss her, to never let her go. Instead, he respected the directive she issued with a slight wave of her hand and stepped back from the microphone.

He wondered if the press noticed the slight tremble of her hands as she gripped the microphone stand and the subtle shift of her body weight from side to side. She was nervous, that much was obvious, and he would've moved to stand beside her if not for that determined glare she'd given him as she'd stepped onto the stage, as if he'd said his piece and now it was her turn.

She cleared her throat once, twice, before tilting her chin up and facing down her biggest nightmare.

'As many of you know I'm Ava Beckett, daughter of Earl Beckett, Australia's recent prime minister. You've written about me for years, reserving a special place in your journalistic hearts for my recent divorce, but I'm here today to give you the latest scoop in the hope you'll respect my privacy later.'

She shot him a quick glance tinged with humour and

truth, and he exhaled in relief, unaware he'd been holding his breath.

'There's been a lot of supposition about my new relationship. Well, I can clear up any misconceptions right now. No, I'm not taking up motor-cross or high wire or bungee jumping, God forbid.'

Uneasy laughter rippled through the room.

'I'm here to be with the man I love.'

Roman's head snapped up as her gaze zeroed in on him and this time he didn't need to analyse anything, her love for him blazing true, turning her eyes radiant blue.

There wasn't a single hoot or catcall or whistle to break the expectant silence.

'Yes, I'm in a relationship with Roman Gianakis, the world's craziest extreme sports fanatic. Yes, I'll be based alongside him, wherever in the world that may be. Yes, I've left the finance world behind and have just accepted a new position as a freelance writer for *Globetrotter*, so...'

Milking the crowd like a pro, she waited till absolute silence reigned before continuing, 'Now you know the latest, people, I want no more scuttle-butt or innuendos, no more free licence to invent what you don't know, just the plain facts.'

She held up a hand to silence the odd disgruntled twitter.

'I know I've been reserved in the past and that hasn't helped my cause. You wanted answers to questions and I deferred ninety-nine per cent of the time. I let my dad and my ex do all the talking for me and you shot me down because of it. Not any more. I'll be more accessible, but only if you respect my privacy and my relationship. Besides, I'm willing to work with you on a more open basis now I'm practically one of you.'

More laughter. Not that he heard much of it. His heart was pounding so damn loud he could hardly hear a thing over its echo in his ears.

'And yes, I promise to give you exclusive updates on our relationship and my other new career as a budding cliff diver on a regular basis.'

A steady buzz filled the room, the murmur of planned questions and she stood there like the queen, her hands steady now, her body relaxed. The din grew as the questions started and, stunned, he watched her answer each and every one, trying to process what he'd just heard.

She was staying.

With him.

As the reality sank in he crossed the few feet between them and wrapped an arm around the woman he adored, something he should've done the moment she professed her love for him to the world.

He covered the microphone with his other hand and bent to whisper in her ear. 'I love you so much.'

'I know.'

'You do?'

She nodded, her impish smile making him want to sweep her into his arms and kiss her senseless, crowd or not.

'Yeah, you wouldn't have ruined your precious reputation in front of these vultures if you didn't.'

'You're awfully confident all of a sudden.'

'Must've rubbed off from you.'

He laughed and removed his hand from the microphone, bringing it to his lips.

'One more question, folks.'

Someone from the back shouted, 'Will the two of you be getting married?'

He expected her to backtrack or fob him off or side-step the question. Instead, she covered his hand on the microphone with hers, eased it towards her and said, 'Damn straight. I need to make an honest man out of him before he flings himself off the next cliff.'

Then she kissed him: in front of reporters, in front of cameras, in front of the world and oblivious to the hooting, stomping crowd, he kissed her right back.

When the roar died down and the paparazzi filtered out, they stepped off the stage and into the shadows of a column.

'Hope that wasn't too *Notting Hill* for you?'

Dazed from the events of the last ten minutes, he shook his head.

'What's the suburb in London got to do with anything?'

Her hand flew to cover her mouth.

'Don't tell me you've never seen *Notting Hill*? Best chick-flick movie ever? Hugh Grant? Julia Roberts?'

He shrugged. 'I'm an action guy. Give you one guess what kind of movies I watch.'

She tapped her bottom lip, pretending to think. 'Better add that to the to-do list: improve Roman's movie preferences.'

'What else is on the list?'

'Oh, the usual stuff.'

She ticked points off on her fingers. 'Move in with Roman. Marry Roman. Live happily ever after.'

'Good list.'

He rubbed his thumb along her bottom lip, giving her a few more seconds' talking before they got back to the kissing.

'But you know I'm not going to give up extreme sports, right? And the paparazzi will always be there, no matter how many exclusives you give them?'

Suddenly serious, she nodded. 'I wouldn't expect you to stop being you any more than I'd want you to expect that from me.'

Sliding her hands around his waist, she hugged him tight.

'As for the intrusive paparazzi, I can tolerate putting on an occasional front when in public with you. Want to know why?'

'Yeah.'

'I went a little crazy when they slandered me for a week straight after my divorce, but it made me realise something. Both my dad and my ex made me feel not good enough, like I was lacking in some way, so I felt like I always had to take a back seat, to let them answer the questions while I put up a reserved front all the time; it was exhausting. With you…'

Her hands slid from his waist upwards, coming to rest on his shoulders as she stared at him with an adoration that made him feel as if he could climb mountains barefoot.

'You make me feel special all the time. You accept me for who I am, you love me for me. Not my name, not what I can do for you, but for me, and that's worth a few "public persona" moments.'

'You're incredible, you know that?'

She nodded, a tear leaking from the corner of an eye. 'I do now, thanks to you.'

As her hands cradled his face and she looked deep into his eyes before broaching the small distance between them and kissing him, he knew right then that he didn't need cameras whirring or flashes popping to feel appreciated.

Love of a good woman accomplished it far better.

EPILOGUE

THE bride and groom hadn't had a moment to themselves for the last month.

Ava Gianakis had been on a whirlwind trip to London to accept her first award for a series of articles on the world's highest peaks.

Roman Gianakis had accompanied her, as she'd tied the articles in nicely to the launch of a new extreme sports school on Hamilton Island, the newest hot spot for adventure-seeking travellers.

They'd met up briefly with Rex, who confessed to meddling in their love lives when he glimpsed sparks between them at their first meeting so arranged to have Ava follow Roman to Hamilton Island on an assignment.

While in London, Ava and Roman had a small civil ceremony, witnessed by Roman's mother, healthier and happier than she'd been in years after a long stint in rehab, and Ava's parents, aiming for incognito in their casual gear.

The best wedding gift? Estelle giving Roman a series of letters from his biological father.

He'd been an English serviceman in the air force, a daredevil pilot who wouldn't settle for anything or anyone. He'd died in the line of fire, doing what he loved best. Roman liked to think he'd inherited his dad's best qualities.

When the happy couple returned to Hamilton Island for their honeymoon, they renewed their vows on their favourite mountaintop.

After the minister departed in a ribbon-strewn golf cart, Roman slid an arm around Ava's waist and hugged her tight.

'I've got a special surprise for you.'

She wrinkled her nose. 'If you expect me to ride down this mountain on the back of a motorbike in this dress, I'll push you off the edge myself.'

'Close your eyes.'

She did as she was told and he pulled a large wrapped parcel from behind a nearby rock.

'Hold out your arms.'

She did and he placed the parcel in them, biting back a grin.

'Go ahead, open it.'

Her eyes snapped open, suspiciously focusing on the package before she ripped the string tying it.

'This better not be what I think it is...'

A crimson sliver of silk poked through the wrapping, followed by tangerine and indigo and brightest daffodil.

Unable to stop the giggles bubbling up, she thrust the package back at him.

'You know I've said no more skydiving a hundred times.'

'But you tried the jump once. And the wake board. And the mountain bike. What's a little jump between husband and wife?'

'Tandem again?'

Enjoying the characteristic teasing of their amazing

relationship, Ava snapped her fingers. 'But only if I get to be on top.'

'Always, my love.'

His lips grazed hers, the briefest of touches having the most profound effect as usual.

'Though there is a problem.'

Anticipating another excuse, he rolled his eyes. 'What now?'

An immense, indescribable joy bubbled up within her.

'There must be some law against pregnant women skydiving?'

He stilled, rigid with shock, before letting out an exuberant yell that must've been heard across the entire island.

'We're having a baby?'

'Uh-huh.'

The dampness in his eyes set off her waterworks as they held each other close and cried.

When he eventually released her, Roman tipped her chin up, his love encompassing her and the baby.

'I love you beyond words. You've given me so much.' His hand splayed across her belly. 'And now this.'

Speechless, he rested his forehead against hers.

'I love you too.'

Her hand covered his. 'Can you believe we're going to be parents? Is there any bigger adrenalin rush?'

He straightened, a tiny frown puckering his brow. 'Hmm.'

'What?'

Jabbing a finger in the direction of the parachute, he deadpanned, 'How small do you reckon they make those things?'

She kissed him to shut him up, something she

planned on doing for the rest of her life. The kissing, that was.

He could coax her to dive the oceans or power down ski slopes, but nothing beat the buzz of loving this man and having him love her back.

She'd found the ultimate adrenalin rush and she intended on getting her fix every day for the rest of their lives.

* * * * *

CLASSIC

Quintessential, modern love stories
that are romance at its finest.

EXTRA

You can find more information on upcoming Harlequin® titles,
free excerpts and more at www.HarlequinInsideRomance.com.

HPECNM0212

REQUEST YOUR FREE BOOKS!

Harlequin *Presents*

PASSION GUARANTEED SEDUCTION

2 FREE NOVELS PLUS
2 FREE GIFTS!

YES! Please send me 2 FREE Harlequin Presents® novels and my 2 FREE gifts (gifts are worth about $10). After receiving them, if I don't wish to receive any more books, I can return the shipping statement marked "cancel." If I don't cancel, I will receive 6 brand-new novels every month and be billed just $4.30 per book in the U.S. or $4.99 per book in Canada. That's a saving of at least 14% off the cover price! It's quite a bargain! Shipping and handling is just 50¢ per book in the U.S. and 75¢ per book in Canada.* I understand that accepting the 2 free books and gifts places me under no obligation to buy anything. I can always return a shipment and cancel at any time. Even if I never buy another book, the two free books and gifts are mine to keep forever.

106/306 HDN FERQ

Name _____ (PLEASE PRINT)

Address _____ Apt. #

City _____ State/Prov. _____ Zip/Postal Code

Signature (If under 18, a parent or guardian must sign)

Mail to the Reader Service:
IN U.S.A.: P.O. Box 1867, Buffalo, NY 14240-1867
IN CANADA: P.O. Box 609, Fort Erie, Ontario L2A 5X3

Not valid for current subscribers to Harlequin Presents books.

**Are you a current subscriber to Harlequin Presents books
and want to receive the larger-print edition?
Call 1-800-873-8635 or visit www.ReaderService.com.**

* Terms and prices subject to change without notice. Prices do not include applicable taxes. Sales tax applicable in N.Y. Canadian residents will be charged applicable taxes. Offer not valid in Quebec. This offer is limited to one order per household. All orders subject to credit approval. Credit or debit balances in a customer's account(s) may be offset by any other outstanding balance owed by or to the customer. Please allow 4 to 6 weeks for delivery. Offer available while quantities last.

Your Privacy—The Reader Service is committed to protecting your privacy. Our Privacy Policy is available online at www.ReaderService.com or upon request from the Reader Service.

We make a portion of our mailing list available to reputable third parties that offer products we believe may interest you. If you prefer that we not exchange your name with third parties, or if you wish to clarify or modify your communication preferences, please visit us at www.ReaderService.com/consumerschoice or write to us at Reader Service Preference Service, P.O. Box 9062, Buffalo, NY 14269. Include your complete name and address.

HP11B

New York Times *and* USA TODAY *bestselling author Maya Banks presents book three in her miniseries* PREGNANCY & PASSION.

TEMPTED BY HER INNOCENT KISS

Available March 2012 from Harlequin Desire!

There came a time in a man's life when he knew he was well and truly caught. Devon Carter stared down at the diamond ring nestled in velvet and acknowledged that this was one such time. He snapped the lid closed and shoved the box into the breast pocket of his suit.

He had two choices. He could marry Ashley Copeland and fulfill his goal of merging his company with Copeland Hotels, thus creating the largest, most exclusive line of resorts in the world, or he could refuse and lose it all.

Put in that light, there wasn't much he could do except pop the question.

The doorman to his Manhattan high-rise apartment hurried to open the door as Devon strode toward the street. He took a deep breath before ducking into his car, and the driver pulled into traffic.

Tonight was the night. All of his careful wooing, the countless dinners, kisses that started brief and casual and became more breathless—all a lead-up to tonight. Tonight his seduction of Ashley Copeland would be complete, and then he'd ask her to marry him.

He shook his head as the absurdity of the situation hit him for the hundredth time. Personally, he thought William Copeland was crazy for forcing his daughter down Devon's throat.

Ashley was a sweet enough girl, but Devon had no desire

to marry anyone.

William had other plans. He'd told Devon that Ashley had no head for the family business. She was too softhearted, too naive. So he'd made Ashley part of the deal. The catch? Ashley wasn't to know of it. Which meant Devon was stuck playing stupid games.

Ashley was supposed to think this was a grand love match. She was a starry-eyed woman who preferred her animal-rescue foundation over board meetings, charts and financials for Copeland Hotels.

If she ever found out the truth, she wouldn't take it well.

And hell, he couldn't blame her.

But no matter the reason for his proposal, before the night was over, she'd have no doubts that she belonged to him.

What will happen when Devon marries Ashley?
Find out in Maya Banks's passionate new novel
TEMPTED BY HER INNOCENT KISS
Available March 2012 from Harlequin Desire!